She halted in confusion just inside his room

Dries was coming from the bathroom, a towel knotted around his waist. He'd obviously just had his shower.

"Oh, sorry," she apologized awkwardly. "I just came to borrow a comb and some toothpaste."

"Help yourself," he said laconically, his eyes narrowing slightly as he surveyed her. "They're on the shelf over the washbasin."

"Thank you," Bryony whispered huskily as she slipped past him, averting her eyes from his strong tanned body. Hastily grabbing the comb, she began to drag it through her tangled curls.

"Changed your mind?" Dries asked softly, coming in and leaning one broad shoulder against the door frame.

"About what?" she asked, staring at him in bewilderment.

"About not fancying fair-haired men."

EMMA RICHMOND says she's amiable, undomesticated and an incurable romantic. And, she adds, she has a very forbearing husband, three daughters and a dog of uncertain breed. They live in Kent. A great variety of jobs filled her earlier working years, and more recently she'd been secretary to the chairman of a group of companies. Now she devotes her entire day to writing, although she hasn't yet dispelled her family's illusions that she's reverting to the role of housekeeper and cook! Emma finds writing obsessive, time-consuming—and totally necessary to her well-being.

Books by Emma Richmond

EMMA RICHMOND

a taste of heaven

Harlequin Books

TORONTO • NEW YORK • LONDON
AMSTERDAM • PARIS • SYDNEY • HAMBURG
STOCKHOLM • ATHENS • TOKYO • MILAN

Harlequin Presents first edition June 1991
ISBN 0-373-11373-0

Original hardcover edition published in 1990
by Mills & Boon Limited

A TASTE OF HEAVEN

CHAPTER ONE

THE house sat, almost defiantly, one felt, in the middle of a large field. It had an air of shabby gentility that was rather endearing, and, glancing down at her old faded jeans and equally faded T-shirt that had miraculously survived too many washes, Bryony gave a faint smile. It must be the first time in her entire life that her appalling dress sense had matched her surroundings, and if this was Dries du Vaal's house, as presumably it was, then maybe the forthcoming meeting wouldn't be as bad as she had anticipated.

Difficult, Daniel had said he was, and wealthy— stinking rich, was in fact how he had phrased it—and he was Dutch. Did he speak English? Yes, of course he must, she thought impatiently. He lived in England , didn't he? It also looked as though he might be eccentric, which didn't exactly bother her. What *was* bothering her was the fact that she didn't know him. It was always so difficult when you didn't know someone!

Chewing worriedly on her bottom lip, she continued to stare at the house. Hauntingly beautiful, with high cheekbones and a pointed little chin, she was ethereal almost, yet surely no ghost ever had laughing grey eyes and a permanent smile. Or normally, that was; there wasn't much trace of a smile at the moment.

A red Ferrari was perched amongst the weeds, which struck something of a bizarre note among so much desolation, and as she passed it Byrony gave it a wary glance, almost as if expecting it to growl at her. Bryony and mechanical devices didn't go very well together.

Pushing through the waist-high grass to the front door, she took her meagre store of courage very firmly in both hands, and knocked. Then knocked again. Nothing. Forcing her way to the window, she peered hopefully in. Not that she could see much—the windows didn't look as though they'd been cleaned for years. With a long sigh, she debated what to do next. Nothing, if the choice were left to her; only she couldn't do that, could she? She'd like to do that, would like nothing better than to go away and pretend he wasn't in. But if she did, she'd only have to come back.

Gazing rather vaguely about her, she wandered round the side of the house. A man was sitting on the flagstoned terrace hunched over a typewriter, and, feeling that calling 'cooee' might be a little out of place in the circumstances, Bryony walked quietly to stand below him.

His proficiency in the art of typing seemed somewhat in question. The same could not be said of his mumbled swearing. That, to Bryony's untutored ear, sounded extremely professional. Always wishing to be charitable, she decided that his difficulty might have stemmed from the fact that both table and chair were tilted drunkenly to one side. Not their fault, of course, when the flagstones were either missing altogether, or hopelessly cracked.

He had a strong face, the nose arrogant, the chin thrusting. Dark blond hair fell untidily across a broad forehead and curled across the collar of his blue denim shirt. Weeds curled across his bare feet, and she had the absurd thought that maybe he'd been sitting there for months while the house and grounds fell unnoticed into disrepair. He also looked as though he wouldn't be very easy to cope with, and Bryony did so need to cope! When he gave no sign of being aware of her presence, she gave a delicate little cough.

'You don't need to emulate a consumptive,' he reproved mildly. 'I'm well aware that you've been standing there for the last five minutes.'

'Sorry,' she apologised inanely.

With a flourishing last peck at the keyboard he slowly turned his head to survey her from beneath straight brows, the same colour as his hair. His eyes were a bright, unwavering blue, and she caught a little flash of surprise in them before he veiled his expression.

'If you've come to offer your services as either a gardener or a cleaner, please don't,' he drawled in a deep, slightly accented voice that was devastatingly attractive.

'Oh, no,' she denied, startled out of her preoccupation. 'I'm Bryony Grant.' When he only continued to regard her with an expression of sorely tried patience, she added helpfully, 'Daniel's sister.'

'Splendid. Now that we've cleared up that little mystery, goodbye. I'm very busy,'

A little smile in her lovely eyes, Bryony climbed up on to the terrace. Terrace? Well, what had once presumably been a terrace, and perched delicately on a large upturned flowerpot. 'You've forgotten who he is?' she asked, puzzled.

'No,' he denied bluntly with another irritable stab at the typewriter keys, 'I never knew who he was,'

'But of course you do!' she insisted, her smile widening, 'He's Clare's friend. I just came to tell you that they've changed their plans and gone to Bangkok early.'

'Early,' he repeated, his attention remaining on his task.

'Yes. Daniel rang me last night, and——'

'Is this going to take long, Miss—er——?' he demanded irritably.

'Grant,' she supplied with a trace of impatience, 'and I find it a little difficult to believe that you can't even remember the name of the boy she went with!'

'Went with where?' he demanded absently, his brows pulled into a frown as he stared long and hard at the piece of paper in the typewriter. With a tut of exasperation, he yanked it out and crumpled it.

'The Far East!' she exclaimed.

'Don't be ridiculous! Clare's in Switzerland.'

'Switzerland?' she echoed blankly. 'How can she be in Switzerland?'

'I don't know!' he burst out in exasperation. 'I haven't the faintest idea what you're talking about! Now will you please go away?'

'But . . .'

With a little gesture of defeat, he leaned back in his chair and stared at her, giving her the benefit of seeing just how bright his blue eyes could be. 'Please?' he pleaded. 'Please just go away. I do not know who you are, I do not know who your brother is, neither do I particularly want to. But what I do know is that my niece is in Switzerland. Now . . .'

'Did she go back today?' Bryony asked hesitantly. It seemed a bit odd, unless she'd had a row with Daniel.

'What the devil does it matter when she went back?' he exclaimed in astonishment.

'Well, I don't suppose it does really. I mean, as long as she's all right.'

'Well, of course she's all right. Why the devil wouldn't she be?' he demanded with an air of aggravated bewilderment.

'No reason, I suppose,' she mumbled dubiously, 'only it just seemed odd, her getting back so soon and everything. If they're seven hours in front . . .' she began, her face screwed up in concentration as she tried to work out the time differences . . . 'that means—that means she won't be back yet,' she concluded, by now thoroughly bewildered. 'I don't understand any of this,' she complained.

'You don't understand any of it!' he retorted, his own face a study in confusion. 'It's a riddle, is that it?' he asked, sounding hopeful.

'Well, of course it isn't a riddle! I've just told you!'

'No, Miss Grant, you haven't. You've given me a long tale of incomprehension which has totally confused me—and, although I'm not normally accused of being slow, I have to confess that in this instance I am completely and utterly at a loss. Now, start from the beginning.'

Mangling her lower lip, her eyes fixed widely on his face, Bryony wondered where the beginning was. 'Daniel, my brother,' she began slowly, 'rang me last night to say they were diverting from their itinerary and going to Bangkok. He said Clare had said you wouldn't care if they went to Bangkok or Timbuctoo, but Daniel thought I ought to know—'

'No,' he said flatly.

'What?' she asked, confused.

'Clare is in Switzerland . . .'

'Don't keep saying that!' she wailed. 'She can't be! With the time difference and everything, if she was with Daniel last night, which would have been this morning there, plus the length of the flight, she couldn't possibly get back to Switzerland until tonight at the latest! She couldn't!' she insisted, then stamped her foot in exasperation when he shook his head. 'Oh, for God's sake! Why would I tell you all this if it weren't true?'

Eyeing her from top to toe, from her curly brown hair that was caught up with what looked like a shoelace into a hastily contrived ponytail, then allowing his eyes to travel over her tiny frame from the well-worn jeans, which were at least two sizes too large, and the grey T-shirt that one got the distinct impression might have started off its life as white, he drawled sardonically, 'Why indeed? Are you an actress?'

'An actress?' she squealed. 'Why would I be an actress? And even if I were, what difference does it make? I came to tell you about your niece, not about being an actress! Really, I knew I should never have got involved, but I——'

'What do you do then?' he asked obdurately.

'I sculpt!' she yelled, exasperated. 'Now will you please ring the school?'

'I don't need to ring the school.'

'Yes, you do!'

'Miss Grant,' he began in a voice that one might use to speak to a retarded child, 'I spoke with Clare only yesterday——'

'Did you ring her?' she demanded.

'No-o, she rang me.'

'Well, there you are, then!' she said triumphantly. 'How do you know she rang you from Switzerland?'

'Because my niece doesn't lie!' he thundered, his patience rapidly running out. Taking a deep breath, he continued more calmly, 'I do not know why your brother should tell you Clare is with him, unless it's someone else's niece named Clare.'

'No!'

'Be quiet! And, so far as I'm aware, Clare doesn't even know anyone named Daniel Grant.'

'Well, that doesn't mean she doesn't!'

'True' he agreed with infuriating condescension. 'However, leaving aside the fact that she might or might not know him, I do know that she's at her finishing school in Switzerland. Now, goodbye, Miss Grant.' With controlled movements, he tipped forward in his chair, wound a fresh sheet of paper into the typewriter, and began to type.

Cupping her chin in her hands, Bryony stared at him defeatedly. 'Please ring the school.'

'Oh, God!' he exclaimed wearily. Resting his elbow on the typewriter and covering his face with his hand, he sat like that for long moments while Bryony fretted and continued to mangle her lower lip until it was sore. As she was beginning to think she'd better try and ring the school herself, he looked up and rested his chin on his clenched fist instead.

'Did your brother tell you to come and see me?' he asked quietly.

'Not exactly. He said he thought I ought to know.'

'He didn't ring you specifically to tell you Clare was there?'

'No. I told you, he rang to say he'd changed his itinerary . . .'

'But he didn't tell you to come.'

'Oh, God give me strength!' she exclaimed weakly. 'I came because I thought you'd want to know. She's seventeen!' she burst out. 'You must want to know where she is!'

'I know where she is! In Switzerland—no, Miss Grant,' he said, holding up his hand when she opened her mouth, 'no more. Please. I don't know what you hope to achieve by this——'

'To make you believe me! That's what I hoped! Oh, well, if you won't, you won't,' she decided, admitting defeat. 'Only don't come grizzling to me when you discover she isn't in Switzerland!' Getting to her feet, she shook her head tiredly. 'Goodbye, Mr du Vaal.'

'Miss Grant, to date this week I've had two girls who looked to be barely in their teens who claimed to have been sent by the producer. I've had one boy claiming to be a friend of Clare's, and who also just happened to be a gardener—and one elderly gentleman who insisted he had a lot of experience of working on a set and would be very happy to be engaged as tea-boy. I've had a very large aggressive woman who desired to clean the house and an ageing alcoholic actor begging for any part at all. So why, Miss Grant, should I believe your tale of incomprehension? Hm? It's different, I have to admit that—and if you hadn't forgotten your lines once or twice I might even have been tempted to believe you.'

Staring at him as though she wasn't sure which one of them had gone insane, Bryony whispered, 'Who are you?'

'Come, come, Miss Grant, you know very well who I am!'

'No, I mean, *who* are you? What do you do?'

Returning her stare, he leaned back again, his eyes narrowed on her bewildered face, and slowly, very, very slowly, his tanned face drained of colour. 'I'll go and ring the school,' he said quietly. Getting to his feet, he walked across the terrace and in through the french doors.

Letting her breath out in a shaky sigh, Bryony closed her eyes, then opened them to stare blindly out across the riot of colour in front of her, not all of it attributable to flowers. Blue plastic sheeting fought a losing battle with a veritable mountain of beer cans in reds and yellows and blues. A rusting green wheelbarrow sat drunkenly in the fishpond—now, she hoped, devoid of fish. The whole place had a sad air of despondency, as though it had finally given up any aspirations it might have had of being a garden a long time ago. Or it had taken its cue from Dries du Vaal.

Why had he asked her all those odd questions? Why did people keep coming to offer their services? Because he was rich? Famous? Yet he'd mentioned a producer, sets, an actor, which would lead one to suppose that he was connected with the film industry. Or the theatre. Was that it? And people came with all sorts of odd tales just so they could meet him? Yet surely telling him his niece was in the Far East couldn't be classed as such a ruse. What would be the point?

Well, Daniel had warned her he was difficult, only she'd thought he'd meant arbitrary. Instead of which he was just confusing, with an air of lethargy that was obviously deceptive. You didn't get to be wealthy, succeed in business, if you were tired all the time, which was the impression this man seemed to give. Or perhaps it was a national trait, she speculated idly, her mind a confused jumble of thoughts, none of which were relevant. Maybe all Dutchmen were large and slow-moving, deceptively languid; whatever, he wasn't at all as she had imagined him. She had expected him to be older, for one thing. She had also expected he would know his niece was in the Far East. And he didn't.

Her shoulders slumping, she hugged her knees. She felt exhausted. 'Oh, Daniel,' she whispered helplessly, 'why do you do these things to me?' Yet obviously Daniel didn't know Clare was out there without her uncle's permission. And when Dries du Vaal found out for sure that his niece wasn't in school, which she couldn't be, what then? He was going to be furious, wasn't he? And who was he going to take that fury out on? Herself, that was who.

Hearing the soft pad of footsteps behind her, she felt herself shrinking, an expression of dread on her small face.

'She isn't there, is she?' she whispered.

'No,' he agreed. 'She told the school I have a serious illness and that she's at home nursing me. That she didn't know when she'd be back. Damn you, Bryony Grant,' he finished softly.

Surprised that a peal of anger hadn't been rung over her head, Bryony turned to stare warily up at him. 'I thought you'd be furious,' she whispered.

'I am furious,' he confirmed.

'You don't look it.'

'No, I very rarely do,' he denied, his voice still soft, reasonable, his expression distracted.

'What are you going to do?'

'Go and bring her back, of course! What else can I do? Maybe I can get her back before Jan finds out.'

'Jan?' she queried.

'My brother, Clare's father! You do actually know where they're likely to be, don't you?' he demanded, making her jump.

'Yes, of course. Bangkok, I said. She'll be all right,' she comforted. 'Daniel will look after her.'

'He'd better!'

'He will!' she assured him hastily. 'He's very responsible.'

'Is he? I don't call persuading a young girl to go off with him to the Far East very responsible!'

'He didn't persuade her!' Bryony insisted.

'Didn't he? How do you know?'

'Well, because he said she just turned up after Easter. In fact he was quite cross about it! He'd hardly be cross if he'd invited her, would he? Oh, God,' she mumbled, feeling drained, 'why did I ever think this would be simple?'

'Simple?' he exploded. 'Right at this moment, emulating an ostrich would be simple! It has a lot to recommend it.'

'I'm not emulating an ostrich!' she said crossly.

'I didn't say you were. Oh, hell,' he added with a tired sigh, 'I really don't need this.' Turning to stare at her, his face thoughtful, he added, 'Well, if you know the name and address of the hotel . . .'

'Oh, yes, Daniel left me an itinerary and everything. Towns, villages, that sort of thing.'

'Do you have the telephone number of the hotel where they're going?'

'No,' she confessed. 'The name's on the itinerary I have at home. I could look it up . . .'

'Never mind,' he denied wearily, giving her a glance of disparagement. 'I'll book us on a flight.'

'Us?' she croaked warily.'

'Yes, Miss Grant—us!'

'But you don't need me!' she protested.

'Ah, but I do. I don't know your brother from Adam.'

'But you don't need to know Daniel . . .' Only Bryony could see from his face that he intended to get to know him—and give him hell. 'It wasn't his fault.'

'So you keep saying—and I can't force you to come, but I would have thought your concern would ensure that you wanted to go. I assumed, obviously wrongly, that your visit here was prompted by concern.'

'It was!'

'Well then, does that concern stop now that you've passed on your fears?'

'No,' Bryony denied helplessly.

'Then you'll come with me.' Swivelling on his heel, Dries du Vaal went back inside and she heard him using the phone again. When he came back out, she stared at him helplessly. 'They're ringing me back,' he told her.

'But I don't know what you think I can do!' she wailed. 'I'm not very good at this sort of thing.'

'You can help me look. If they aren't at this hotel, then obviously we'll have to track them down—you know your brother, how his mind works . . .'

'Well, you know your niece—don't you?' she asked, confused all over again.

'No,' he said bluntly. 'Jan had to go off at a moment's notice on a lecture tour in the States. He rang me to ask if Clare could come to me for the holidays. Asked me to keep in touch with her, make sure she was all right. Hah!' he exclaimed with a look of self-contempt, 'he's only been gone five minutes, and now look at me!'

'But you know what she looks like . . .'

'Well, of course I know what she looks like—from photographs! The last time we actually met face to face was three years ago! None of my damned family ever seem to be in the same place at the same time!'

'Oh,' said Bryony flatly.

'Yes, Miss Grant, oh. I know very little about her, what she does, how she behaves—witness this little fiasco.'

'But if neither you nor her father knew she was going, how did she afford it?'

'Because Jan gives her unlimited bloody funds! Oh, God,' he said suddenly. 'How are they travelling?'

'Backpacking.'

'Not hitch-hiking?' he asked in horror.

'No,' she denied, not knowing anything of the sort, only there was no need to worry him more than was necessary, was there? 'Buses, trains, that sort of thing. Daniel wanted to see the world before he went to university. Took a year off,' she explained. 'And I'm sure——'

'How old is he?'

'Eighteen. He's nice,' she murmured inconsequentially.

'I'm quite sure he is,' he retorted. 'Any boy that can persuade a young girl to go off with him to the Far East has got to be nice!'

'That's not fair!' she exclaimed. 'He didn't persuade her, or even invite her. She just turned up! He said she did!'

'Don't be ridiculous! Clare wouldn't dump herself

on someone without invitation!'

'How do you know? You said you didn't know her.'

'I don't, but I can't imagine Jan and Lilly bringing
her up to behave like that. They're probably the most
strait-laced pair I've ever met!'

'Then that's probably why! Rebellion! And if they
hadn't let her have all that money——'

'Oh, a psychologist, are we?' he asked sarcastically.

'No, of course not! But seventeen-year-old girls
aren't children! In fact, they're often a great deal more
worldly-wise than I am!'

'Hardly difficult,' he derided, then shook his head
in a sort of apology. 'Sorry, fighting with each other
isn't going to solve anything. How long has he known
her?'

'Not long. They met in Paris just after Christmas.
He presumably told her about his plans for this year—
and I think they kept in touch. She'll be all right,'
Bryony murmured, turning to face him. 'He'll look
after her and everything.'

'Yes, I'm sure he will,' he agreed, looking as though
he didn't think any such thing. 'It's the looking after
her that's worrying me.'

'What's that supposed to mean?'

'Don't be naïve! Clare's a very beautiful young
woman—at least, she looked as though she was from
the last photographs I saw of her, and no young man
worth his salt is going to stick to a platonic
relationship, is he?'

'Well, that doesn't say a lot for your niece, does it?'
she asked, incensed. 'And I'd be enormously grateful
if you wouldn't judge Daniel by yourself! Oh!' she
exclaimed, putting a hand across her mouth.
'Sorry—that was presumptuous.'

'Yes, wasn't it?' Removing her hand and holding it loosely in his own, Dries du Vaal stared down at her, his eyes narrowed. 'So the mouse has teeth, has she?'

'Mouse?' she queried, cross all over again.

'Mm, you look like a very bewildered mouse. Or you did. Now I'm not so sure.'

'Thank you,' she said sarcastically. Then, tilting her head to one side in a listening attitude, she mumbled, 'I think the phone's ringing.'

Tilting his own head, he nodded. 'Probably the travel agent.' Releasing her, he turned to pad inside, Bryony following at his heels.

Her eyes fixed on his face as she listened to the one-sided conversation, she suddenly grabbed his arm. 'Don't we need visas and things?' she whispered urgently.

'What? Oh, hang on a minute,' he said impatiently into the phone, then covering the mouthpiece, he asked, 'What?'

'I said don't we need visas and things . . .'

Giving her a harassed look, he uncovered the phone and asked about visas. 'No—yes—all right—yes, two tickets. Thanks, we'll pick them up at the airport.' Replacing the phone, he stared down at Bryony. 'We don't need visas or injections—well, we probably do,' he grumbled comically. 'The way things are going, we'll no doubt end up with yellow fever, but they aren't compulsory. We take off at five-thirty.' Taking her elbow, he propelled her out on to the terrace, where he continued to regard her thoughtfully. 'Do you always leap so readily to your brother's defence?'

'No, but you keep insisting it's his fault, and it isn't.' Staring up at him, her eyes even more troubled, Bryony wondered if she ought to warn him of the reaction he was likely to get if he accused her brother of kidnapping his niece. Daniel wasn't very reasonable when people accused him of things. He never tried to justify himself, explain. If he thought he was in the right that was all that mattered to him. She had tried to explain to him that it was sometimes better to give explanations, because people did tend to misconstrue his behaviour, to absolutely no avail. Daniel didn't actually care what people thought of him. She did, so perhaps it was just as well she was going, she decided despondently. At least she could try and ensure fair play.

'Did he know Clare was out there without anyone's permission?' Dries du Vaal demanded.

'No, of course not! He would have said.'

'Then why didn't he ask you to come round here to tell me they were moving on?'

With a big long sigh as she debated whether to tell him the truth or not, Bryony finally explained, 'Because he didn't think I'd do it.'

'Why ever not?'

'Because I never do anything that's liable to prove troublesome,' she confessed awkwardly.

'So why did you now?'

'Because she's only seventeen! And I thought you might be worried if she wasn't where you thought she should be!' And I know what it's like to be seventeen and all alone in a strange place, she thought despondently. 'He will look after her,' she repeated, and if she said it often enough perhaps she'd come to believe it herself.

'All right, give me half an hour to get ready, then we'll be off. Make yourself a cup of tea or something,' he added absently before padding back inside.

With a funny little sigh, Bryony went to find the kitchen. The house looked a bit like hers—untidy. Washing herself up a cup from the stack on the draining-board, she boiled the kettle and made herself a cup of tea, then walked back out to the terrace. Sitting in the chair Dries du Vaal had so recently occupied, she wondered why she was being such a lame-brain. She didn't want to go to the Far East. Certainly she didn't want to go with Dries du Vaal. He was disturbing, she thought with a frown. And she didn't want to be disturbed; she never did. So why don't you just go and tell him you're not going? she thought. Because it smacked of being uncaring. And because despite her championship of Daniel, telling Dries he was responsible, she wasn't terribly sure that he was. If he got fed up with Clare whinging on, as he put it, wasn't he just as likely to dump her? Then justify his actions by saying he hadn't invited her?

'Oh, Daniel,' she whispered helplessly, 'please look after her,' Letting her breath out on a long fluttering sigh, she stared down into her cup.

'Having second thoughts, Miss Grant?' Dries asked softly from beside her.

'No,' she denied despondently, 'I was just thinking.' Then as his words registered properly, she gave him a look of disgust. 'How can I have second thoughts when you didn't let me have any first ones?'

Squatting down beside her, he stared into her gentle face. 'I thought you might be wondering how wise you were being, rushing off to the other side of the world with a man you barely know.'

'No —or maybe yes,' she contradicted herself, 'just a bit, only I decided you didn't look the sort of man to like mice,' she added with an air of hopeful expectancy as though daring him to even think he might.

'No,' he agreed as he continued to examine her exquisite face. 'Is there anyone who's going to worry about you? Parents? Boyfriend?'

'No,' she said baldly.

'No boyfriend?' he asked in surprise.

'No.' And you can make of that what you like, Mr Dries du Vaal, she thought defiantly. If he thought she was going to tell him all about herself, he was in for another think!

'You said that as though you hated men,' he observed softly. 'Do you?'

'No, of course I don't. I just . . .' I just can't cope with them, she completed mentally. Or they can't cope with me, which amounts to the same thing, doesn't it? 'Do you? Have a girlfriend who won't like you going with me, I mean?'

'Think she might be jealous?' he taunted.

'No. Why should she be jealous? I'm hardly a *femme fatale*, am I?'

'Aren't you? I begin to wonder,' he said pensively.

'Oh, come on!' she exclaimed with a little flash of alarm in her eyes. 'Don't start that. I'm only coming at your insistence, certainly not because I fancy you or anything . . .'

'Oh, good,' he drawled, his eyes narrowed. 'Why?'

'What do you mean, why?' she asked, astonished. 'Or do you expect every woman who meets you to fall at your feet? Fine conceit you have if you do!'

'No,' he denied, not looking in the least embarrassed by her outburst, 'I was merely trying to ascertain whether you were going to be a problem.'

'Well, I'm not! I'm never a problem! I'm the most amiable person I know. Anyway,' she added in sudden inspiration, 'I like my men slim and dark-haired, not fair-haired giants!'

'Hardly a giant,' he denied, a small smile tugging at his mouth. 'Still, it's comforting to know your taste runs in an entirely different direction.'

'Yes,' muttered Bryony, averting her eyes from his strong face. Yet what exactly was her taste? She was hardly a connoisseur. In fact it had been a hell of a long time since she'd even been out with a man. Turning her head, she gazed rather sadly out over the garden. And whose fault was that? Dragging her mind back to the present, she faced Dries again, a rather haunted look in her eyes. 'Can you just take time off like this?' she asked.

'Fortunately, yes. Can you?'

'Yes, which is just as well, isn't it?' she asked with a touch of asperity, 'seeing that you didn't give me a choice.'

'There's always a choice,' he argued absently. 'You don't have commissions and things?'

'Sometimes,' she confessed, 'although I don't have anything outstanding at the moment. Usually I just do something I want to do, and if it sells, fine, if it doesn't . . .'

'You don't give a damn,' he finished for her. 'Yes, I'm beginning to get quite a good idea of the ways of Miss Bryony Grant.'

'I doubt it,' she contradicted with a little gleam of humour in her eyes which seemed to surprise him. Tilting her head on one side, she asked curiously, 'Why did you ask me if I was an actress?'

'It's not important.' Then, much to her own surprise, his own eyes crinkled with humour.

'Why so secretive?' she asked. 'What do you do?'

'Special effects. I set the scene, so to speak.'

'Films? Television?'

'Mm,' he said vaguely.

'Oh, you thought I'd come to try and get a part in one of your films? Is that it?'

'Something like that, yes,' he agreed.

'But I didn't —only that's why you just asked me if I was going to be a problem, isn't it?' Bryony continued thoughtfully, her eyes fixed widely on his face, 'because now you know I know, I might——'

'Mm,' he interrupted, his eyes amused.

'Are you famous?' she asked. 'Should I have heard of you?'

'No, and probably not, not unless you read the credits, do you?'

'Oh, no, I don't watch films or television, or not very much anyway,' she denied dismissively, as though she couldn't understand why anyone else would either.

With a wry smile, Dries got to his feet.

'Are we ready?' Bryony asked uncertainly.

'Well, I am, certainly. I'll just put these things inside.' Picking up the typewriter as though it weighed no more than an ashtray, he carried it in through the french doors. Cup in one hand, the chair in the other, Bryony followed him. Well, at least she'd cleared up the question of why he'd considered she might be a problem, she thought in relief. For a while there, she'd been quite worried, because she didn't want to be a problem, not to anyone. All she wanted was to find Clare and then come home again; certainly she didn't want any involvement with Dries du Vaal. And he was a giant, she thought—at least, compared to her five feet three he was.

As he passed her in the doorway, going back out to collect the table, her mind still revolving with his words, she asked, 'How tall are you exactly?'

'Six two. Is it important? Did you want your dark-haired man the same height? Smaller?'

'No,' she argued, surprised by his sarcasm. 'I don't want a man at all. I was just thinking that if you were shorter, you'd look stocky.'

'Oh, I see. How fortunate I'm not shorter, then. I would so hate to be accused of being stocky.' Shaking his head, he went to get the table.

'I only meant . . .' Bryony began, then shrugged, not sure how to explain she hadn't meant her remarks personally.

'What?' asked Dries softly, halting in front of her, the table held like a barrier between them.

'That I'm interested in form, from an artistic point of view. You know, shape, texture . . .'

'Mm.' Giving her another odd look, he carried the table inside.

Not sure if she'd been believed, Bryony followed.

When he had locked the doors, he ushered her out into the hall. 'How did you come?' he asked. 'Car?'

'No, I can't drive. I came on the bus and then walked.'

'Where do you live?'

'Not far, actually. The other side of Sevenoaks—Eynsford.'

'OK. Off you go, then.' Practically pushing her out of the front door, Dries slammed it behind him, then tossed his bag into the back of the car. Opening the passenger door with a flourish, he closed it after before walking round to the driving seat. 'Put your seatbelt on— I drive fast.'

'I didn't think it was allowed,' she remarked, doing as he said.

'It isn't. But providing there's no traffic in the lanes, and providing I can see a good way ahead, I drive fast. Why? Are you nervous?'

'No, I don't think so. Would it make any difference if I was?'

'Probably not. We have a lot to do and very little time to do it in. How long will it take you to pack?'

'Not long. I had a shower and changed before I came to see you. All I have to do is toss some things into a bag, and I'll be ready.' Bryony smiled faintly at the pained look that crossed Dries's face. 'Were you hoping I might dress up?' she asked softly.

'No,' he denied drily, 'I'd already come to the conclusion that hope should be abandoned.'

And if you stay like that, Dries du Vaal, I can cope, she thought, her spirits lightening. If he would remain good-humoured and amiable, it would be all right. Relaxing back in her seat, she closed her eyes. With luck they could fly out, find Clare, and fly back.

When he drew up before her little detached house that stood in its own acre of ground, she eyed it somewhat more critically than previously. She had to admit it didn't look a great deal tidier than his garden, minus the beer cans, of course. When they went inside, she gave a rueful smile. Her house didn't look any tidier either. 'Good job we don't live together, isn't it?' she grinned.

'You just lost me again, I'm afraid,' he told her, closing the front door behind him.

'The muddle we both live in, I mean. We'd never find anything, would we?'

'I don't live there!' he exclaimed, sounding

positively outraged. 'It's for a film set. I've been working there trying to turn it into a haunted house!'

'Oh.' Feeling foolish, Bryony gave him a placatory smile, then indicated that he should go into the lounge. 'My passport and Daniel's itinerary should be in the bureau, if you'd care to rummage while I go and pack,' she instructed, before turning and running lightly upstairs, a small smile tugging at her mouth for her mistake. Unfortunately, she thought ruefully, she couldn't claim any valid reason for the untidiness of her own house!

Dragging her old rucksack out from the bottom of her wardrobe, she debated a few moments on what to take. Clean underwear, shorts? Oh, why not? It would probably be hot. A couple of T-shirts. Scrabbling through the bottom drawer of the bureau, she came across a pair of cotton trousers she hadn't actually worn, and with a thankful smile, she thrust them into her rucksack. Sweater? Yes, it might be cool in the evenings, they'd obviously be there for at least one. What else? Groping round in the bottom of her wardrobe, she found her Indian sandals and pushed them in. That should do it. Last, but by no means least, she carefully put her large and small sketching pads and a selection of pencils on top. Sitting back on her heels, she thought furiously— money, she'd need money. Perhaps Dries would stop at the bank—what was the time? Oh, hell, where was her watch?

Grabbing her rucksack, she went back downstairs. He wasn't where she'd left him. Seeing the open door to her workshop, she felt a *frisson* of alarm; she didn't like people going in there, not even Daniel. Dumping her rucksack on the floor, she walked swiftly to push the door wide. Unlike the rest of the house, this room was obsessively tidy. Dries was standing in front of the large window, examining one of her figurines.

'Yours?' he asked softly.

'Mm,' she mumbled warily.

'Mm,' he echoed. 'One could forgive you a lot for work like this. It's excellent.'

'Thank you.' And what the devil did he mean by 'forgive'? As far as she was aware she hadn't done anything that needed forgiveness.

Picking up her rather flat tone, he asked in surprise, 'You sound angry. Are you?'

'No, I . . .'

'Hell, Bryony, I'm sorry. I'm intruding—is that it? You don't like people in here?'

'Something like that,' she murmured with a helpless shrug. 'I didn't mean to be rude. I'm a bit defensive, I suppose.'

'But why? My God, if I could do work like this I'd invite all and sundry in just to show off!' Dries told her.

'That I strongly doubt,' Bryony said wryly, but his easy acceptance made her relax. 'I'm a bit of a perfectionist and I suppose I expect people to find fault.'

'Yes, I can understand that.'

'You can?' she asked, surprised.

'Of course. I may not have a talent like yours, but like you I constantly expect criticism of my efforts, then, when it's not forthcoming, I'm surprised.' Smiling at her, the first really natural smile he'd given, Dries looked back at the figure in his large hands. 'What is it?' he asked.

'Applewood,' she told him absently.

'Applewood? I didn't know you could carve that.'

'Didn't you?' she asked, walking across to take it from him. Staring down at the figure of the naked young girl and the expression of shy modesty that she had managed to capture on the exquisitely detailed face, she explained quietly, 'Grinling Gibbons always used applewood. There's a fine example of it at Warwick Castle. It isn't easy, certainly, but very rewarding.'

Smiling down at her, his eyes wryly amused, Dries taunted softly, 'Are you famous?'

'Heavens, no! I usually manage to sell what I make, but I do it because I love doing it. It's the only thing I've ever wanted to do.' Replacing the figurine on the window-sill, she asked, 'Did you find them?'

'Did I find what?'

'My passport and the itinerary.'

'Oh no, I haven't looked yet. Sorry.'

'OK, I'll find them. I also seem to have misplaced my watch.'

Frowning slightly, Bryony walked back into the lounge, and, crossing to the bureau, yanked it open. Papers and photographs cascaded to the floor in a veritable flood. Anyone else would have exclaimed crossly and attempted to pick them up. Not Bryony; she ignored them, left them where they fell, and it was Dries who with wry exasperation hunkered down and began collecting them together.

'Ah!' she exclaimed triumphantly. 'Here they are. Passport, and itinerary.' Suddenly catching sight of what he was doing, she waved her hand vaguely at him. 'Just shove them all back in. They aren't important.'

'Until presumably you need something else.' Doing as she said, he took her passport from her and put it with his in his back pocket. Unbothered, Bryony walked across to the table and spread the itinerary out.

'What date is it?' she asked absently as she ran her finger down the list.

'The twenty-fifth.'

'May?'

'Yes,' he said somewhat impatiently. 'Don't you even know what month you're in? Here, let me see.' Edging her to one side, he read down the list with growing disbelief. 'Delhi, Agra, Jaipur, Jaisalmer, Jodhpur, Kathmandu, Kashmir, Goa, Hong Kong, Bangkok—dear God, Bryony, is he possessed of a small fortune?' When she didn't immediately answer, he turned his head to look at her.

Gazing at him, a look of helplessness intermingled with humour on her small face, she gave him a lame smile. 'Er—yes. Disgusting, isn't it?'

'And he's blowing it all on travel?'

'Oh, no,' she exclaimed unthinkingly. 'I told you, he's travelling quite cheaply, public transport and all that . . .' then she tailed off lamely at his expression of incredulity.

'And are you possessed of an equal fortune?'

'Oh, no, Daniel keeps me,' she told him blandly, her eyes innocently wide, because that wasn't any of his business either.

'Hm,' he said drily.

'But I can afford to pay my own shout,' she reassured him. 'Can we stop at a bank on the way to the airport?'

'Yes,' he muttered. Still staring at her as though not quite sure what to do with her or about her, he asked,

'How did you know where to find me?'

'Daniel gave me a telephone number that he'd made Clare give him when she first went out, in case of accidents, or emergency, and—well, the girl who answered said you were staying just outside Westerham, and gave me the address.'

'Oh, did she?'

'Only, I think, because I'd said it was to do with your ward,' Bryony added hastily, not wanting to get the girl into trouble.

'Mm. Oh well, come on—but I have the very gloomy feeling that I'm going to regret this,' Dries told her.

'You can always cancel my ticket,' she offered hopefully.

'No.' And he headed firmly for the door.

CHAPTER TWO

THEY called in at Bryony's bank to collect some
traveller's cheques, where Dries also purchased some,
then on to Heathrow, where he parked his car in the
long-stay car park before ushering her across the ramp
to the concourse. He took charge, collected and paid
for the tickets, presented their passports and
proceeded to the boarding gate just as the other
passengers were being herded outside, and Bryony
wondered whether things always ran so smoothly for
Dries du Vaal. They never did for her.

Boarding the aircraft, and taking the window seat at
Dries's urging, she stared rather blindly from the
window. Fourteen hours, she thought. She'd forgotten
that—that she would be forced into close proximity
with this rather disturbing man. It had been a long time
since she had felt this tug of attraction for anyone, not
since David, in fact, two years before, and it wouldn't
do, she thought, impatient with herself. It really
wouldn't do. Not that Dries was likely to feel the same,
but even so, she would have to be on her guard.

'What's wrong?' he asked quietly. 'Afraid of
flying?'

'What? Oh, no,' she denied, swinging to face him.
'Just thinking.'

'About what? Your brother?'

Shaking her head, Bryony took out the lifejacket
instruction leaflet from the pocket in front of her and
pretended to read it. She'd been a bit naïve, she

supposed, thinking she wouldn't feel attracted to a man, just because she didn't want to be. It seemed so simple in theory . . . Oh, for goodness' sake, she told herself scornfully, as she thrust the leaflet back in the rack, pull yourself together! Just bury the hunger along with the regret! Treat him as a brother—or a Dutch uncle, she thought with a little twitch of her lips.

When the in-flight magazine was plonked forcefully into her lap, she blinked, startled out of her preoccupation, and turned to look at her companion.

'You've been muttering and fidgeting like someone in the last throes of dementia!' he exclaimed impatiently. 'What on earth is the matter with you?'

'Nothing. Sorry.' Bryony apologised lamely, 'I get a bit fidgety with nothing to do.' With a faint smile for his aggrieved expression, she explained humorously, 'I'd forgotten it was such a long flight.'

Handing him back the magazine, she bent to retrieve her sketchbook and a pencil from the rucksack. 'I'll be creative,' she announced decisively. 'That will keep me quiet.'

As soon as the seatbelt sign winked out, she unhooked herself, twisted in her seat so that she could see the passengers across the aisle, and met the eyes of a rather supercilious young woman just across from Dries. She was looking at Bryony as though she couldn't believe her eyes. With a wicked little smile, Bryony began to draw a caricature of her.

'That isn't very nice,' Dries reproved when he saw what she was up to.

'I don't care,' she shrugged. 'I don't like the looks she keeps giving me.'

'They probably have something to do with the way you're dressed,' Dries observed with a faint smile.

'So I gathered.' Looking up at him, she asked teasingly, 'Does it bother you? Will you be embarrassed carting me around?'

'No, and no. I very rarely get embarrassed.'

'No, that's what I figured. You look as though you don't give a damn what anybody thinks anyway.'

'I don't. Is that liable to occupy you until we land?' he asked, indicating her drawing.

'Probably not. Why? Not expecting me to entertain you, are you?'

'No, why should I expect you to entertain me?' he asked, sounding astonished.

'No reason, but if you did, you'd do better to talk to the lady across the aisle. She looks as though she'd be more than happy to oblige.'

'Miaow!' grinned Dries.

'Not a bit of it,' Bryony denied airily. 'I was merely trying to be helpful.'

'Well, don't.' Staring rather thoughtfully at her sketch, he asked slowly, 'Can you draw other things, apart from faces?'

'What sort of things?' she asked, puzzled.

'Rooms. May I?' Without waiting for her answer, he took the pad and pencil, and, turning to a clean page, began to sketch the layout of a house. 'That sort of thing,' he explained, showing her.

Thrusting out her lower lip while she thought about it, she gave a little nod and took the pad back. Tearing his page off and crumpling it, she dropped it absently in his lap. 'The house where you were working?'

'Mm.' Leaning over her shoulder, he described the layout he had in mind, and as she competently sketched in the detail he asked idly, 'You love it, don't you—drawing?'

'Yes,' she confessed, 'I always have. Sometimes whole days go by without me even noticing, when it's going right, that is, a bit like a writer's flow, I suppose. You know?' When he nodded, she continued, 'Sometimes all it takes is a deft stroke here and there to capture what I'm trying to achieve and I have to clench my hands to stop myself "improving". Other days nothing will go right. I imagine you find much the same thing.'

'Yes. Pity we can't tap into inspiration to order,' he agreed absently. 'Staircase winds to the right,' he instructed, his eyes fixed on what she was doing, then with no variation in tone he asked, 'Tell me why your brother's rich.'

'Grandfather left it to him,' Bryony explained.

'But not to you?'

'No, don't be silly. I was a girl, and Grandfather didn't have a very high opinion of girls. Rails or struts?' she asked, pencil poised to draw the banister.

'Struts. One can see why, if your grandmother was anything like you,' Dries retorted mildly. 'Why wasn't it left to your parents?'

'Grandfather didn't like them. Or, more precisely, he didn't like his son, my father. One can't blame him. Daniel and I didn't like him much either.' Leaning back, her pencil held idly in her hand, Bryony gave a faint smile. 'I often think that was why I took up sculpting—it was the dirtiest profession I could think of.'

'Explain,' he directed drily. 'I don't think I've ever met anyone who so loved to talk in riddles!'

'Well,' she began, not averse to launching into a saga of her family history, 'first of all, it was a great disappointment to my parents when I turned out to be

a girl. A shame really, because I was rather sweet . . .'
Ignoring his grunt of laughter, she continued,
'Being—well, sort of quite pretty, I suppose,' she
added with an awkward little twitch, 'I was dressed in
pretty dresses, white usually. And I wasn't allowed to
get dirty. No playing in the garden for me. No mud
pies, no mixing with the other horrid dirty children.
My mother was also rather puritanical, and as soon as
she decently could she carted me off to a convent
school where she assumed I'd be safe from the horrors
of the world. Boys, she meant.'

'Did it work?' asked Dries.

'I shan't tell you. When I was nine,' she continued
firmly with a fascinating little smile, 'Daniel was
born.'

'You're twenty-seven?' he exclaimed in
astonishment. 'Good grief, you don't look more than
eighteen!'

'And act it, I think you were about to add at that
point,' she teased with a little look at him under her
lashes. 'Well, and so I do, sometimes. It probably has
something to do with a repressed childhood.'

'It doesn't seem to bother you much,' he remarked.

'No, I don't think it does. Well, not now, at any rate.
It did then. Lord, but I was miserable! Anyway, to cut
a long story short, when Grandfather died—who, by
the way, was Loring Grant—I——'

'The industrialist?' asked Dries.

'Yes, and as my father was his only child, and
Daniel his only grandson, it all went to Daniel. Father
was furious! However, there was very little he could
do about it.'

'And you got nothing?'

'No. Anyway, two years after that, the parents were

killed in a car crash and Daniel came to live with me in a poky little rented room in Scotland. The trustees let him have enough of the money to live on —to pay me rent, actually, because I could barely afford to keep myself, let alone Daniel, and it all worked out very well,' Bryony finished airily.

'I don't believe a word of it,' muttered Dries, folding his arms across his chest and staring at her.

'No, no, it's all true,' she insisted lightly—and so it was, sort of. It was her feelings on the matter that were different —because she did mind, she always had, but you had to keep the demons at bay, didn't you? Anyway, they were only chance-met acquaintances and she couldn't think Dries was even remotely interested in her family history. Unless it was to discover what sort of influence Daniel was likely to have on his niece. Turning to look at him, she saw the stewardess poised beside him, coffee-pot in hand. 'I think you're wanted,' she said softly. 'You shouldn't have let me ramble on so,'

'How does one stop you?' he asked drily before turning to smile at the stewardess. 'Black, please, no sugar. Bryony?'

'Oh, white, three sugars.' She grinned when they both looked at her in astonishment. Flipping down the little shelf that served as a table, she put her coffee on it before handing Dries the pad. 'Will that do?' she asked.

'Mm, that's fine. May I borrow the pencil?'

Handing it over, she watched him make little crosses all over it. 'X marks the spot for special effects?' she queried.

'In theory,' he agreed. Frowning down at it, much as he had on the terrace, he began to write.

Instructions, she supposed.

'Tell me about you,' she encouraged, picking up her coffee and sipping it.

'What's to tell?' he asked with a humorous little shrug. 'My life story would be very dull by comparison.'

'Nonsense! Tell me why you're stinking filthy rich, as Daniel put it. Tell me where you got that tan, tell me——'

'All right, all right,' he agreed, abandoning his writing. 'I got the tan in Mexico, I'd been out there filming since February.'

'Do you have to stay on the set, then?' she asked curiously.

'Yes, usually, unless it's pretty straightforward, which isn't necessarily the case.'

'What were you filming?'

'Oh, a sci-fi thing, lots of flying saucers and aliens,' he explained offhandedly.

'And you have to construct them? Make them work?'

'Yes. Line up camera angles to create the best illusion.'

'Do you enjoy it?' asked Bryony.

'Of course. I wouldn't do it if I didn't.' With an intriguing little smile, his eyes lightened with rueful humour. 'We usually have great fun. Like a lot of schoolboys, especially when we have to construct something to be exploded, nice lot of big bangs,' he enthused, and when she smiled back, easily able to picture him laughing gleefully as they blew something up, he added softly. 'It also pays very well.'

'Which is why you can afford to go haring off to Bangkok.'

'Yes,' he agreed, his smile dying.

Regretful that she had introduced a sombre note when she'd been enjoying their exchange, Bryony consoled him, 'She'll be all right.'

'Yeah.' With a long sigh, Dries leaned back and stretched out his long legs.

'What training would you need to have to become a special effects person?' she persevered.

'What? Oh, engineering degree, something like that. Or just an ability to make things, clever handiwork. Why? Thinking of applying?'

'Heavens, no! I don't think I could bear to blow something up that I'd just lovingly created.'

'No, but there's a vast difference between your creations and mine,' he pointed out. Returning his attention to the pad, he frowned down at it for a moment, before continuing with his writing.

Staring at him, at the strong-boned profile, Bryony gave a rueful smile. And she'd been worried he might find her disturbing? She doubted if he even remembered she was there. Shaking her head, she turned to look from the window. The rest of the flight passed without any other such confidences being exchanged, and, after the meal had been served and cleared away, she tilted her seat back and tried to sleep. With a bit of luck, this time tomorrow they would be on their way home.

Bangkok was hot, steamy and noisy. Feeling slightly disorientated by the fact that it was late afternoon instead of the early morning her body insisted it was, Bryony climbed tiredly into the taxi outside the airport. Pushing the already damp hair off her forehead, and squinting up at the bright sky, she asked quietly, 'Is it always this hot?'

'It's usually pretty humid,' Dries confessed absently as he stared around him, 'Why? Does the heat affect you?'

'I don't know, I've never been anywhere this hot.' It certainly didn't seem to affect him, she thought, feeling suddenly lonely and excluded. He looked as though he hadn't even noticed. Probably he was thinking about Clare, or his complicated special effects.

Leaning back against the seat, she tilted her face to catch all the breeze there was going, her mind drifting as she anticipated the surprise Daniel was going to have when they met. She just hoped Dries would use a bit of diplomacy. She gazed out of the window, the sights and sounds gradually giving her thoughts a new direction, and she busily scanned her surroundings, examined faces as they blurred past. Not that she expected to see Daniel, of course—no one could be that lucky—and after a while she forgot to even look at the people, there was so much else to see. Domes gilded by the sun, three-wheeled taxis that appeared to be on a suicide Derby and the little tuk-tuk noises they made, made her laugh and yearn to try and capture it all on paper.

'Isn't it amazing? Exactly as you imagine it,' she pronounced in surprise. 'Noisy, colourful, crowded— oh, hey—look!' she exclaimed, craning from the taxi window. 'Canals!'

'*Klongs*' said Dries repressively. 'They're called *klongs.*'

Turning to stare at him, worried and a little puzzled by his odd attitude, she saw the humour in his eyes, and smiled in relief. 'You've been here before,' she accused.

'Yes,' and, with a small smile of his own, he obligingly pointed out some of the sights to her, most of which seemed to involve temples, or *wats*, as he loftily informed her. 'If we have time I'll take you to see the Temple of the Emerald Buddha, it's pretty impressive. And here we are at the hotel,' he added drily, 'which, happily, is air-conditioned.'

As soon as they had registered and been shown up to their adjoining rooms, Bryony walked across to fling the shutters wide. Elbows on the sill, chin in her cupped hands, she stared out into the sprawling city below. Was Daniel walking out there somewhere? Having a high old time? She hoped he was, hoped he was looking after Clare. Conjuring up a picture of her brother's face, she gave a faint smile. He had worked so hard to get his A levels, get into university which he would be starting next September, had so looked forward to this well-deserved break, and she didn't want anything to spoil it for him. She wanted to go out there, find him, warn him—only Dries had told her to stay put until he called for her. Retreating from the window, she went to unpack her rucksack. Feeling sticky and crumpled, she collected clean underwear and went to have a shower.

Wrapped in the little silk kimono that had thoughtfully been provided for guests, she hunted in her rucksack for her toothbrush and a comb, before remembering that she hadn't actually put them in. She didn't have any toothpaste either, or else she could maybe have used her finger. Sitting back on her heels, she ran her tongue round her teeth. They felt coated and horrible. Maybe Dries would let her borrow his.

Leaving her door open, she walked along to his

room and, giving only a perfunctory knock, pushed the door wide. He was just emerging from the bathroom, a towel knotted round his hips, obviously just having had his own shower, and she halted in confusion.

'Oh, sorry,' she apologised awkwardly. 'I just came to see if I could borrow a comb and some toothpaste.'

'Help yourself,' he said laconically, his eyes slightly narrowed as he surveyed her. 'They're on the shelf over the washbasin.'

'Thank you,' she whispered huskily as she slipped past him, keeping her eyes firmly averted from his strong tanned body. Half naked, he wasn't in the least chunky, she thought inconsequentially as she hastily scrubbed her teeth, using his toothbrush— in fact he was beautifully in proportion. A smooth broad chest that tapered to a narrow waist, long, muscular legs, a faint down of hair on the shins . . .

'Can't you find them?' he asked, walking into the bathroom behind her.

'What? Oh, yes, yes, thank you. I hope you don't mind, but I used your toothbrush. I'll buy you a new one.' Hastily grabbing the comb, Bryony began to drag it through her tangled curls, uncaring for the moment of the pain she was causing herself.

'Changed your mind?' Dries asked softly, leaning one broad shoulder against the door-frame.

'About what?' she asked, staring at him in bewilderment.

'About not fancying fair-haired men.'

Her mind for the moment unable to comprehend his meaning, she simply stared at him, and when he lifted one eyebrow in amused query the penny dropped. 'You think I came because——No!' she exclaimed in shock. 'I came to borrow your comb! I said so!'

'So you did.'

'I did!' she insisted. 'And I don't find it in the least amusing for you to pretend otherwise!'

'Pretend?' he echoed.

'Yes, pretend! I told you I was only coming to help find Clare, and I did. Not for any other reason whatsoever!'

'Then why the scanty attire?'

'Certainly not for your benefit!' she exclaimed, horrified that he should assume any such thing. 'I didn't stop to think . . .'

'Then you should have done. Wandering half naked into a man's bedroom is a damned dangerous occupation! You don't know me, don't know anything about me. I could be——'

'Yes, you could—probably are! But not to me!' she interrupted hastily as she gave a stubborn knot a furious yank that brought tears to her eyes.

'As it happens, no, but that doesn't —oh, what on earth are you trying to do?' Dries demanded in exasperation, as she encountered another stubborn tangle. 'Scalp yourself? Here, give it to me.' Walking across to her, he removed he comb from her. Pushing her into the bedroom, he made her sit on the edge of the bed and perched behind her. With incredibly gentle movements that were so at variance with his impatient tone, he began to untangle her hair.

'I didn't, Dries,' she began worriedly. 'Honestly. I never even considered what you might think.'

'Then that makes you even more dangerous,' he said reprovingly.

'I'm sorry,' she mumbled, 'but I'm so used to wandering into Daniel's room, or him into mine, that I didn't give it a second thought.' Do you ever? she castigated herself.

'There you are,' Dries said, quietly handing her the comb.

'Thank you.' Getting quickly to her feet, Bryony hovered awkwardly for a moment, her troubled eyes fixed on his face.

'You're too thin,' he observed as he glanced down at the long length of leg exposed by the short kimono.

'I know, I forget to eat. I'll go and get dressed, shall I? And then we can go and look for Daniel and Clare. Or should we try ringing their hotel first?'

'If they're there.'

'They will be,' she said positively, profoundly thankful that they were back on safe ground. 'Daniel will stick to his itinerary—he never deviates. If he has a plan, then the plan is strictly adhered to —well, it will be now,' she qualified hastily when Dries gave her an old-fashioned look, remembering that this whole muddle had occurred because Daniel hadn't stuck to his itinerary.

'No,' he denied, still looking thoughtful, 'we'll walk round there, it isn't far.'

'Why didn't we book into the same hotel?' she asked curiously.

'If you'd seen the hotel, you wouldn't ask,' he retorted drily.

'Why? Is it a bit . . .?'

'To say the least. It's not one that tourists normally go to, but cheap. And the Lord only knows why they want to pig it when they could easily afford to have rooms with a decent bed and a bathroom with water that actually comes out of the tap!'

'No,' Bryony agreed lamely, because she didn't know why either. 'Perhaps they hadn't known what it was like when they booked it.'

'Perhaps.' Rolling to his feet in one fluid movement, that made Bryony take a hasty step backwards, which seemed to amuse him, Dries stood in front of her. 'Are you really as insouciant as you appear? Aren't you even the slightest bit worried about Daniel? Eighteen is a bit young to go traipsing round the world.'

'I suppose it is, only Daniel has never seemed very young,' she murmured reflectively. 'He always behaves as though he's older than me —and, as I said before, he's very sensible, very self-sufficient, and as long as he keeps in touch, I don't worry about him.'

'Mm.' His expression changing, Dries trailed one finger down her cheek, making her shiver. 'You know, you really are an astonishingly beautiful woman. Beautiful bones. Doe's eyes . . .'

'Does have brown eyes,' she contradicted quickly, taking another step backwards. 'Anyway, I'm too thin—you said so.'

'Yes, but it doesn't detract from your beauty. And that husky voice does things to a man that it really isn't very wise to do. Go away, Bryony Grant, and let me get dressed. I'll call for you in a few minutes.'

With a jerky little nod, she escaped. Her hands to her hot cheeks, she wasted precious moments while she considered his flattering remarks. She didn't want to do things to Dries that he didn't want done, husky voice or no, she thought in a rather frantic fashion. A flirtation with Dries du Vaal was the last thing she wanted. He didn't look very easy to cope with—and if there was one thing Bryony valued above all else, it was her need to cope. If there was a situation that she knew she wouldn't be able to handle, then she avoided the situation, which made it doubly stupid for her to have gone half naked into his room. She'd been rather treating Dries as though he were another brother—and, as he had pointed out, that could be dangerous, or stupid. Or very wise? she wondered. Well, she'd be very careful not to do anything so daft again! Terrified he would arrive to collect her before she was ready, she scrambled into the blue trousers and a clean T-shirt.

When Dries called for her some ten minutes later, he seemed preoccupied and to her relief made no mention of her earlier behaviour. Taking her arm with a gesture she didn't think he was even aware of, he led her out into the warm, noisy afternoon, and Bryony gazed curiously about her, anxious to give her thoughts a new direction. Bangkok seemed a fascinating mixture of ancient and modern, seamy-looking side-streets and brightly lit thoroughfares, she thought as Dries led her through a confusing maze of streets. He obviously knew where he was going, so Bryony allowed her gaze to travel where it would—shops spilling out on to the pavement with their tantalising, different wares, temples, and a surprisingly large number of gold-leafed statues of elephants.

'You might even see some real ones,' Dries promised with the air of a kindly uncle as he noticed her entranced expression, and she chuckled.

'Do they really come into the city?'

'Oh, yes. Like any other country, there's a high rate of unemployment, even for elephants and their *mahouts*.'

'Their keepers,' she interpreted knowledgeably. 'They spend their whole working lives together, don't they? Elephants and their keepers grow old together.'

'So I believe,' he agreed, giving her an indulgent smile, his earlier preoccupation obviously forgotten or resolved. 'But with the teak forests being slowly denuded, there's not the work for them that there was. That, unfortunately, is progress.'

'Yes,' she said sadly, 'and when it's too late and all the forests are deserts because there are no longer any trees to hold the topsoil in place, there'll be no need for elephants at all—or even people. We don't deserve this lovely planet, do we?'

'No, Bryony, I don't believe we do.'

Halting before one of the statues, Bryony pressed some of the flapping gold leaf back with a thoughtful finger. 'Did you know that elephants are some of the best swimmers in the animal kingdom?' she asked softly, and didn't see his amused smile. 'They use their trunks like snorkels. I like elephants' she announced abruptly with a firm little nod of her head.

'Oh, good.'

Turning to look up at him, seeing his bright amused glance, she grinned and hugged his arm. 'I know I said I didn't want to come, but I'm glad I did, aren't you?'

'Glad that you came, or that I did?' he teased.

'Both.'

Giving her one of his warm lazy smiles, he agreed softly, 'Yes, I rather think I am—although I could have wished it were in different circumstances. Come on, we'd better get on.'

Trying to look everywhere at once, Dries's hand firmly on her arm, they continued through the narrow, crowded streets, and their slow pace had the advantage of allowing Bryony to examine some of the goods they passed. Exquisite material, exotic foods, fruits, birds in cages. If it wasn't for their mission, she could have spent hours happily wandering round. The people, who all seemed amiable in such a crush, unlike London where everyone got grumpy, were a mix of races, mix of costume and speech. Momentarily parted from Dries, because she did tend to lag when she went anywhere, Bryony halted to stare at some exquisitely carved ivory until he grabbed her and moved her bodily out of the way of a car as it tried to thread its way through the throng of people.

'I do wish you'd watch where you're going!' he snapped.

'Sorry,' she apologised absently.

Hot and breathless as he resumed tugging her down side-streets, perspiration trickling uncomfortably down her back, she was enormously glad when they reached their objective. Or at least, she would have been if it hadn't looked so seedy. Dries had said it was cheap, but this place looked as though it wouldn't have been able to give the rooms away! The paint on the red front door was chipped and peeling; the stone façade cracked, shabby, and she looked at Dries worriedly, expecting a little homily on her brother's inconsideration in allowing Clare to stay here. When none was forthcoming, just a frowning look, she followed him in through the open front door, then hastily retreated again. Whew, the inside was like a Turkish bath! It was hot outside, but infinitely preferable to being in there. She might be a lot of things, she thought, but masochist wasn't one of them. She'd wait outside. Dries was more than capable of making enquiries on his own.

When he was gone longer than five minutes, she began to wonder if he had in fact found the couple and was even at that moment giving Daniel a hard time.

Her little face determined, she was just about to go back in when she caught a fleeting glimpse of a dark head, a backpack. Turning curiously, she was suddenly galvanised into action.

'Daniel!' she screeched. Forgetting all about Dries and her need to stay put, she plunged into the narrow, crowded alley, desperately trying to keep the dark head in sight. Pushing, apologising, squeezing herself through gaps, frustrated by her lack of height, she frantically called Daniel's name, which it was doubtful anyone would have heard in that noisy throng. Seeing the dark head just in front of her, she made a last desperate lunge and grabbed the back of the rucksack, dragging him to a halt. Laughing, out of breath, she wriggled her way in front of him—and stared into the startled face of a complete stranger. And not even an English complete stranger!

'*Madame?*' he queried. '*Qu'est-ce qu'il y a?*'

'Oh, she said lamely.'*Non. Pardon*—er— *excusez-moi.*' Her schoolgirl French quite unequal to the task of explaining, she gave him a sheepish smile. 'I thought you were someone else . . .*Pardon.*'

With a little shrug and another puzzled look, he continued on his way.

With a disappointed little sigh, Bryony turned to go back—only to discover that she hadn't the faintest idea which way back was. Staring round her in bewilderment, she began to walk in the direction she thought she had come from, only she didn't quite remember that it had been an alleyway of jewels. Frowning, she tried to remember any identifying landmarks that she might have seen on her way in—she also suddenly remembered Dries. Oh, heavens, he was going to kill her! With a little sound

of exasperation for her stupidity, and for lack of any
other bright ideas, she wandered along the alley in
front of her. At first she only absently returned the
smiles and nods she received; shook her head at
traders who all tried to persuade her to come inside, to
buy the incredibly cheap small rubies and sapphires
that were on display. And over everything seemed to
be the smells of spice, flowers—and unwashed
humanity, she had to admit, wrinkling her nose.

Unfortunately, by the time she reached the silver
stalls, the batik work, silks, satins, cottons, she had
become thoroughly diverted from her urgent need to
find Dries. Her footsteps slowing yet further, she
stopped to examine some of the exquisite work-
manship. And it just had to be, she thought
vexatiously, that Dries would spot her at the very
moment she was laughing at something the stallholder
had said to her. It couldn't have been when she was
looking worried or panicky—oh, no, he had to wait
until she looked as though she didn't have a care in the
world. Staring at him, she swallowed nervously. He
looked furious, and hot, and she felt a stab of guilt.

'What are you doing?' he asked coldly.

'I . . .'

Holding up his hand, his voice barely raised, just
quietly savage, he castigated, 'You have got to be the
most selfish, irresponsible person it's ever been my
misfortune to meet! I've been scouring this market for
what seems like hours, and I'll tell you here and now
that I have no intention spending half my time
searching for your irresponsible brother and the other
half searching for his equally irresponsible sister! And
if you ever, ever do that to me again, I'll kill you!
Anything could have happened to you! Anything!

Now move!' Grabbing her arm, he thrust her ahead of
him, then prodded her painfully in the back when she
remained still.

'Dries!' she exclaimed, turning to look mournfully up
at him. 'I didn't—wasn't! I thought I saw Daniel . . .'

'I don't give a damn what you thought you saw! Any
more than you gave a damn when you left me not
knowing what the hell had happened!'

'Not on purpose!' she denied, her worried eyes
searching his implacable face.

'Did you leave a message for me?' he demanded.

'Well, no . . .'

'Did you give me even one single thought?'

'Yes! But if I'd come into the hotel to tell you, I'd
have lost him!'

'So where is he?' he asked nastily, giving an
exaggerated look around.

'It wasn't him,' she confessed. 'But it might have
been! And I couldn't take the chance that it wasn't!
Dries,' she pleaded unhappily, 'please don't be cross!'

With a look of disgust, he turned on his heel and
began to walk away.

'Dries!' Afraid of losing him, of getting lost all over
again, Bryony ran to catch him up. Grabbing hold of
his sleeve, she brought him to a halt. Standing in front
of him, she stared up into his stony face. 'Please don't
be like this,' she entreated. 'I was only trying to help,
and then I got lost. I'm sorry,' she apologised
contritely, then gasped with pain as he caught her arm
in another punishing grip and shook her,

'Do you have any idea what you put me through?
Do you?' he demanded, 'I thought you'd been
kidnapped, abducted——'

'Don't be silly! Who . . .?' Lapsing into silence at

the look of fury he gave her, she lowered her eyes. Whatever she said would only exacerbate his temper further. She would do better to keep her mouth closed.

Swearing under his breath, Dries began dragging her through the market as though she were a naughty child, and Bryony's temper began to simmer. She didn't lose it very often, but enough was enough. She'd apologised, for goodness' sake! What did he expect her to do? Grovel?

When they reached a wide thoroughfare, he hailed a taxi, then ruthlessly shoved her into the back before climbing in beside her.

'Were Daniel and Clare all right?' she asked stiffly, her face set.

'I wouldn't know! They weren't there.' His own face totally devoid of expression, he added harshly, 'They stayed one night, then wanted to leave. The clerk recommended they try the Dusit Thani.'

'Oh, I didn't know,' faltered Bryony.

'Well, why didn't you damned well ask him when he rang you? You told me you knew which hotel he was staying at!'

'Well, I thought I did! And anyone would think I'd deliberately misled you, the way you're carrying on! It was the name on his itinerary!'

'Which he doesn't deviate from!' Dries snapped sarcastically.

'Oh, for heaven's sake!' Clamping her lips firmly together, Bryony leaned back and gave a long sigh. 'Well, let's hope they're at the Dusit Whatsit now,' she prayed fervently, otherwise he was likely to strangle her. Turning her head, she glared at his stern profile. 'You do look it,' she muttered disagreeably.

'What?'

'Cross. You said when you were cross, you didn't look it.'

'Oh, shut up!' he exclaimed wearily.

With a little sniff, she glared at the back of the taxi-driver's head. 'Are we going to the Dusit thingy now?' she asked, curiosity finally getting the better of her.

'I'll go there now. You'll stay in the taxi.'

The rest of the journey to the Dusit Thani hotel was completed in silence.

'Wait here. And I mean here,' stated Dries with a little glare of his own as he got out. Explaining slowly to the driver, who only had a little English, he gave Bryony another warning glance before going into the hotel. He was only gone a few minutes, and when he came back he looked ten times more furious than he had when he had when he went in. A short spat she could cope with; prolonged aggression made her feel sick.

Without speaking, Dries got into the cab and instructed the driver to take them back to the New Imperial.

'They aren't there?' Bryony eventually plucked up the courage to ask.

The look of disgust he gave her successfully precluded her from asking anything else.

'Get packed,' he said curtly when he had collected their keys.

'Where are we going?' she queried.

'Butterworth.'

Where on earth was Butterworth?

Staring at her, taking in her white face, her wide unhappy eyes, he muttered, 'It's in Malaysia. We have to get the overnight train.'

'Oh,' said Bryony flatly.

'Yes, oh. Really sticks to itinerary, doesn't he?'

Unable to think of anything to say, even remotely in mitigation, she just stared at him.

With a soft oath, Dries thrust her key into her hand and stalked off towards the lift.

She was tired, hungry, and she felt sick, which meant she wouldn't be able to eat anything even if she was given the opportunity, which she didn't think she would be. She hadn't done any of her shopping either—and she needed to! 'Dries,' she called hesitantly after him, 'do I have time to do my shopping?'

'No,' he said, stepping into the open lift without turning round.

'But I need some things,' she whispered helplessly. Eyeing the closing lift door, then the street, she felt a little spurt of defiance. It wasn't as if she'd wandered off without a reason! He hadn't even tried to understand! Her face mutinous, she determinedly retraced her steps. This was the only opportunity she was likely to get, and if she didn't take it . . . She'd noticed a dear little shop almost next door to the hotel that seemed to sell everything from dresses to soap. If she was quick . . .

CHAPTER THREE

CAREFULLY rolling up the two cotton shift dresses she had bought and stuffing them down the side of her rucksack, Bryony eyed the other parcels despairingly. She'd never get them all in. Oh well, perhaps Dries wouldn't notice she had more luggage than she'd started with. Anyway, she didn't care if he did! It was his own fault for being so poky. She was damned if she was going to keep feeling guilty! He was the one who'd insisted she come!

For once being quite efficient and actually checking that she hadn't left anything behind, she went back down to Reception to wait for Dries. Except that Dries was already there before her. The minute she arrived, he stalked out of the hotel, and she had to run to keep up with his long strides.

They took a taxi to the station, and again Dries walked off, leaving her to follow. Juggling her parcels, her face set, Bryony scurried along the platform after him. She did hope he wasn't going to turn into one of those people who sulked!

'Look,' she muttered breathlessly as she trotted to keep up with him, 'this is getting ridiculous! I've said I'm sorry, and I am. It won't happen again.'

'It looks to me as though it already has,' he said shortly, and she looked at him in exasperation.

'Well, so it did,' she confessed crossly, 'Which you wouldn't have known about if I'd managed to get everything into my rucksack!'

'Which doesn't alter the fact that you deliberately disobeyed me.'

'Dries!' she exclaimed, coming to a halt and throwing the crowds behind her into confusion, 'I'm not a child! I'm quite capable of looking after myself! I admit I was in the wrong earlier——'

'Big of you.'

Staring at him, exasperation darkening her lovely eyes, she suddenly saw how ridiculous they were being and gave a snort of laughter. With a hop and a skip to catch up with him again, she shook her head in disgust. 'Boy, you can be so wrong about people. You seemed so laid back too.'

'Laid back?' he exclaimed, coming to an abrupt halt and doing some crowd confusing of his own. 'What a revolting expression!'

'Well, yes, I expect it is, but you seemed so lethargic and—well, amiable,' she explained.

'Lethargic? I work damned hard!'

'I didn't say you didn't! Just that you seemed——'

'Lethargic—yes, you already said,' he said coldly.

'And that you didn't get cross.'

'I didn't say anything of the sort! I said I didn't look cross!'

'Well, you look cross now,' she pointed out, 'and I do wish you'd stop sulking, it makes me very uncomfortable. I hate rows and arguments and people being cross with me. I can't cope.'

'You can't cope?' Dries asked incredulously.

'No. And would you please tell me how we're supposed to fit into a train that already looks packed to bursting point?'

'We're travelling first,' he said with an arrogance that didn't become him in the least. 'If we must go chasing all over the Far East, I at least intend to do it in comfort. If you want to squash in with the masses, that's entirely up to you. Unless of course you can't cope with that either,' he added.

'Don't be pompous!'

'I feel bloody pompous!' he shouted, and then looked so comically surprised by his outburst that she burst out laughing. After a few moments' struggle, his lips twitched, then widened into a rueful smile. 'You're a wretched girl,' he told her ruefully.

'I know. Friends again?' Bryony asked entreatingly. Although it might actually be better to remain at odds with him, at least it drowned out the attraction she kept feeling. Yet, contrarily she didn't want him to be cross with her, she wanted it to be how it was.

With a long sigh, Dries shook his head at her, before exclaiming on a laugh, 'Oh, do stop looking at me as though I'm going to beat you! I'd like to beat you, but I won't.' Taking the parcels out of her arms, he walked another few steps before halting again. 'Go on, in you go.'

Peering into the compartment, Bryony blinked in astonishment. It was quite empty. 'How long are we on the train for?' she queried.

'Twenty-four hours.'

'Twenty-four hours?' she squeaked, 'Good grief! I don't mind roughing it, Dries, but surely this is rather going to extremes?' Climbing obediently in, she then gave a little crow of delight as the guard pulled down two concealed bunks. When he had departed, mumbling something she didn't understand, she perched on one of the beds. 'I thought perhaps we were supposed to sleep on the floor,' she said.

'No.' Staring down at her as she perched like a little bird on the long cushion, her feet clear of the floor, Dries sighed again. 'I'm beginning to understand why you told me you wouldn't be much help—you aren't safe to be let out on your own.' Tossing her packages down, he sat opposite her.

'Don't be misled by my looks and actions,' she reproved gently. 'I'm really quite resourceful. Sometimes.' With a small smile, she picked up her parcels. Sorting through them, she handed him one. 'I bought you a present,' she murmured, her face bland.

Taking it, shaking his head at her, he opened the neck of the bag and peered inside, then gave a little grunt of laughter. 'Oh, Bryony, what am I going to do with you?' Taking it out, he held the Mickey Mouse toothbrush and stand on the palm of his hand. 'What's this? Subtle reproof for behaving like a child?'

'No, of course not,' she denied softly. 'It was all they had. I've got Goofy.'

'Figures,' he retorted drily. 'What else have you been buying?'

'Chef shoes.'

'Chef shoes?' he echoed.

Picking up another bag, she opened it and took out the soft little black canvas shoes and held them out for his inspection. 'Chinese chef shoes. You can't get them in England. They're really comfortable.'

'They look like old gym shoes,' he commented, taking one of the tiny shoes in his large palm.

'Yes, but the soles are softer. Haven't you ever noticed? Chinese people always seem to wear them— because they're so comfortable, I expect. And incredibly cheap.'

'And small,' he said softly. 'My, Grandma, what small feet you have!' he taunted.

'Size three. And I do wish you'd stop treating me as though I were a child!' she reproved.

'It's safer,' said Dries wryly. 'Tell me what else you've been buying.'

Deciding for once in her life to be sensible and not ask him why it was safer, Bryony explained, 'Toothpaste, toothbrush, hairbrush, and a couple of cotton dresses. Now tell me where we're going.'

'Penang.'

'Thank you.'

'You're welcome.' And Bryony grinned, happy now that good relations had been restored. 'Daniel and Clare booked out of the Dusit Thani yesterday morning,' Dries told her.

'Then how do you know . . .?'

'Because,' he explained, rather grudgingly she felt, 'your brother told the desk clerk where they were going. So when I got back to my room, I rang the hotel they're going to, to leave a message for them to stay put until we arrive.'

'Sensible,' she approved.

'Well, I thought so.'

With a little gurgle of laughter, she curled up on her seat. 'But they are all right?'

'I suppose so—yes, they're all right,' he agreed. 'We'll catch up with them tomorrow and then fly back.'

Nodding, she settled back, then gave him a startled look as the train lurched and began to move. For a moment she had forgotten they were actually going anywhere. Getting to her feet, she went to stand at the window. There was something rather fascinating about watching a train pulling out—or being on the train that pulled out and watching the platform.

Unfortunately, the fascination didn't last. By the time they had been through the rigours of the air-conditioning that froze them both, the passport control and Customs, fascination had long since departed. Even the sight of the thick jungle encroaching on the track, or the monkeys swinging almost within reach and the endless paddy fields, failed eventually to enchant her. And as for the toilet arrangements, they were the stuff of which nightmares were made! She hadn't exactly expected Hilton standards, but she had expected something a little more modern than a hole in the train floor.

By the time they neared their destination, she was cold, tired, because she hadn't slept very well, and hungry. Even though food had been brought to their cabin, it hadn't looked very appetising and she had left most of it.

'How much longer?' she asked, pushing her tangled hair off her forehead.

'Another hour, I guess. Why don't you go and have a wash and freshen up?'

'OK.'

Washing as best she could with mud-coloured water that seemed reluctant to flow, and trying to keep her balance at the same time, proved to be a test Bryony felt quite unable to pass. After only the sketchiest of washes, she bundled up her toilet things and made her way back along the swaying train. Smiling automatically at an elderly gentleman burned nearly black by the sun, she didn't have the heart to walk on when he seemed so pathetically

eager to talk to her, and then she became so
fascinated by his tales of his life in the Far East she
only just made it back to the compartment before
they pulled into the station.

'I was just about to send out a search party!' Dries
exclaimed in exasperation.

'Sorry, I met an Englishman in the corridor,' she
explained absently, 'Do you know, he's lived out here
nearly all his life! Imagine that, never once going back
to England.'

'Just imagine,' he taunted, and she poked her tongue
out at him. 'Do you talk to everybody?' he asked as
they collected their belongings together.

'It certainly seems like it sometimes,' Bryony
agreed with a small smile. As she watched him,
watching the economical movements that were so
fascinating in such a large man, her smile widened.
She was glad she had come, glad to have met him; he
was a nice man, she decided, and it was always a bonus
to be comfortable with someone, even if he was rather
disturbing. But she was coping with that all right,
wasn't she?

After the cool air in the train, the heat of Butterworth
hit her harder than she had expected, and she was more
than glad when Dries escorted her on to the ferry to
cross to the island of Penang. At least it created some
sort of breeze. They then took a trishaw to the E & O
hotel in Georgetown, and Bryony instantly fell in love
with it. The hotel stood in lush lawns that sloped down
to a sea that sparkled aquamarine in the sunshine.
Jacaranda and hibiscus fought with frangipangi and
bougainvillaea, and she inhaled their scents almost
dreamily. The original old colonial building had been

added to over the years, yet, oddly, the newer buildings didn't detract from the overall sense of age and tranquillity. 'Oh, Dries, it's perfect!' she sighed. 'Is this where they're staying?'

'No. I couldn't get us into their hotel, it was full—however, it isn't far away. Come on, the sooner we get registered, the sooner we can go and find them and go home.'

'Yes.'

'Well, don't sound so disappointed! It's why we came!'

'I know,' she agreed softly.

'You could always stay on after I've taken Clare back,' Dries pointed out.

'Yes, I suppose so. Oh, well, I'll think about it,' she said, knowing she wouldn't. It wouldn't be the same on her own.

Taking her arm, he led her into the reception area, then smiled at her enthusiasm when they were taken into the old part of the hotel. A young boy, who looked to be no more than nine, carried their bags, and, opening the door of Bryony's room first and putting her rucksack on the bed, he opened the french doors that opened out on to the lawn. With a wide smile, obviously delighted by her pleasure, he went out with Dries's bag.

'We'll have a wash and brush-up and something to eat before we go,' said Dries. 'I'll see you in a few minutes, Bryony.'

Flapping an absent hand at him, she stayed staring out into the grounds as Dries went into his own room.

With a rather forlorn hope that the creases might out, Bryony changed into one of the cotton dresses she had bought in Bangkok, then, unable to find anything to tie her hair up with, filched a piece of the tassel that held the curtains back before joining Dries in the pleasantly cool dining-room. Unaware of the startled glances she was receiving for her rather odd appearance, glances that very quickly changed to humour, she stared round her in delight at the lingering essence of a bygone age. She could almost expect a portly gentleman in a panama hat, wiping his face with a white handkerchief, to appear and immediately order a pink gin.

'We'll go and see Daniel and Clare before I book a flight home,' said Dries, 'and then if there's time we'll take the bus round the villages and I'll show you the nutmeg and rubber plantations, the cloves——'

'You're being very nice and indulgent,' she teased, her head on one side as she observed him across the table.

'Mm, must be the balmy air—make the most of it. Besides,' he added lazily, 'if I give Clare a little treat, she might be more amenable to going back to school.'

'Oh, I see. I should have known it wouldn't have anything to do with me,' pouted Bryony.

'So you should. Ready?'

'Yes.' Wiping her mouth with the snowy white napkin, and smiling at the Malay waiter, who beamed happily back, she followed Dries out.

'Why are you laughing?' she asked, slippping her hand into the crook of his arm.

'Because you're so delightfully unaware.'

'Unaware of what?' she queried.

Coming to a halt, Dries stared down at her. 'You don't even notice, do you?' he asked softly, using one finger to push a stray wisp of hair aside. 'Everyone in the dining-room was dressed to the nines and in comes Bryony, totally oblivious of the sensation she's creating, dressed in a cheap cotton smock that looks as though it's been packed in someone's trunk for years . . .'

'But it's cool,' she protested solemnly, her lovely eyes alight with laughter. 'Did I embarrass you?'

'No, not in the least—I think I'm beginning to enjoy it. Being seen with you doesn't do my ego any harm at all. Even oddly dressed as you are, I think you're the most feminine woman I've ever met. Your every gesture is dainty, delicate, the way you hold your head, smile——'

'Oh!' she exclaimed, embarrassed, her hands to her hot cheeks. 'What a lovely thing to say!'

'Is it?' he asked, smiling down at her.

'Yes. Thank you. And I don't at all believe you have an ego,' she added.

'Don't you?' With an odd smile, he gave her a little tug. 'Come along—and perhaps I should also mention,' he continued, slanting her a teasing look, 'that you're disruptive, aggravating, and——'

'Stop right there!' she exclaimed, laughing. 'Let me keep some illusion that I'm desirable.'

'Oh, you're desirable,' he murmured, coming to another halt. 'Unfortunately.'

Staring at him, feeling the sudden tension that crackled between them, Bryony turned and hastily walked on.

Georgetown was fascinating, she told herself firmly, shutting everything else out of her mind. It was—oriental, that was it. And what else would it be? she asked herself scathingly. Everywhere she looked there were Chinese . . .

'Calm down,' Dries said softly, catching hold of her arm and slowing her. 'Rushing about in this heat, you'll make yourself ill.'

Obediently matching her steps to his, she resolutely kept her face averted, pretending complete absorption in the wayside stalls and the poky little buildings they passed. Fool, Bryony! she scolded herself. That was just plain daft, teasing him, laughing with him—flirting with him, almost. Won't you ever learn?

'Oh, this is ridiculous!' Dries exclaimed softly, and she turned to look at him in wary surprise.

'What is?'

Bringing her to a halt, he stared down into her bewildered face. 'This is.' Moving his palms up to frame her face, he bent and swiftly kissed her. Moving back, he watched for her reaction, his eyes bland.

'What did you do that for?' she demanded, more startled and confused than she would have thought possible.

'Lord knows,' he sighed, his eyes lightening with mocking laughter. 'I probably just wanted to see if it solved anything. It didn't. Now come along before I forget all my good intentions.'

What good intentions? she wondered blankly. Touching her mouth with her fingertips, she glanced at him worriedly as he tugged her along the narrow street. A little frown in her eyes, she tried to persuade herself that he was just being friendly. All the same, it was a good job they were going home today.

The hotel at least proved to be an improvement on the one in Bangkok, and this time, Dries made sure Bryony went inside with him. While he made enquiries at the desk, she watched him, puzzled about what he had meant. Was he attracted to her? And instead of the shaft of panic she should have felt at such a possibility, all she had felt was wistful. Could she change? she wondered. With a long, rather sad sigh, she decided she couldn't. Getting involved with a man had never worked before: why should it now? With an odd feeling of impending doom, she turned away to look round the foyer. As she examined some of the wall carvings, one finger tracing hideous masks, delicate ladies in strange and exotic costumes, her mind kept straying to might-have-beens.

'Well, they certainly booked in here yesterday morning . . .' Dries began, his face and voice reflecting his abstraction.

'And?' she asked fatalistically.

'And the clerk I spoke to wasn't on duty when they arrived,' he added.

'So they didn't get your message?'

'He isn't sure. The message is no longer in their box, so he thinks they probably got it—'

'But he can't say with any certainty. So now what do we do?'

'Go back to our hotel and wait for them to contact us. I might have known, mightn't I?' Dries asked in disgust. 'I really might have known. Oh damn! What's the matter with you?' he asked, peering intently into her face. 'You look thoroughly distracted.'

'Nothing,' she denied hastily. 'Just thinking about something else. Did you leave another message?'

'What? Oh, yes, telling them where we were staying. Are you sure you're all right? It's not the heat getting to you, is it?'

'No, of course not,' she said impatiently. 'Clare was

with him?'

'Yes,' he agreed absently as he continued to stare down at her.

'Well, thank goodness for that!' she said fervently. Giving him a brilliant smile to cover up the fact that he was making her feel very uncomfortable by the way he kept staring at her, she added stupidly, 'Thank you.'

'What did I do?' he asked, poking back another errant strand of hair that had escaped her peculiar topknot.

'I don't know. Looked after me, I suppose. I don't think I would have done very well if I'd been on my own.'

'Despite that resourcefulness you were telling me about?' he teased. 'Although I doubt your journey would have progressed much further than Bangkok,' he added wryly. 'Getting side-tracked is a definite failing of yours, Bryony Grant—and where on earth did you get that strange-looking ribbon that isn't coping very well with keeping your hair in place?' he added.

Profoundly thankful that he was now behaving normally, Bryony led the way outside before admitting. 'From the tassel on the curtains in my room. I didn't think they'd notice one little bit missing.'

'No, I don't suppose they will. And even if they did, you'd charm them into not minding. Wouldn't you?'

'Would I?' she asked in surprise.

'Yes. Come on, we'll get a taxi—I'm not totally convinced you're not suffering from the heat. We'll laze around the hotel gardens, conserve our energy until they turn up.'

That sounded suspiciously as if he thought they'd

need a lot of energy when they did turn up. Why? Did he know something she didn't 'All right, ' she agreed, 'and perhaps I ought to get myself a hat. Oh, hey, look at that!' she exclaimed.

Turning in the direction she was pointing, Dries enlightened her. 'It's the Kek Lok Si Temple—seven tiers, if you care to count. I believe it's called the Pagoda of Ten Thousand Buddhas—and no, I do not want to go and visit it. Not at the moment anyway. It's too hot.'

'Spoilsport! And what's that hill I can see?'

'Don't know,' he admitted, 'except I've only ever heard it referred to as Penang Hill. I believe there's a funicular that goes to the top. However, I personally am rather in favour of a swim. Yes?'

'Yes,' she agreed, smiling at him, 'seeing that you're such a lousy tourist guide.'

'We aren't here as tourists,' said Dries severely. 'Did you bring a swimming costume with you?'

'No,'

'Then we'll go and buy some swimming gear, then go and laze by the hotel pool.'

'Isn't there a beach at the hotel?' asked Bryony.

'No, There are any number of nice beaches around the island, Batu Ferringhi being one of them. Not that I think you'd want to join the smart set . . .'

'Dressed like this?' she grinned, noticing that the creases hadn't fallen out, as she had known they wouldn't.

'I didn't think you cared what you looked like,' Dries explained.

'I don't. But I thought you might.'

'Not me,' he denied. 'Come on.'

Suddenly, to her utter astonishment, without any

warning at all, it rained. Water just fell out of the sky as though a bucket had been emptied. With a shriek of surprise, Bryony ducked beneath a nearby awning, then laughed delightedly when Dries refused to hurry and only continued to saunter casually to join her.

'Must be four o'clock,' he said solemnly, slanting her a look, seemingly quite unbothered by his soaked state or the water dripping down his face from his saturated hair.

'Why must it be four o'clock?' she asked obediently.

'Because in Malaysia it always rains at four o'clock, just a light shower. It will be over in a few minutes.'

'Now isn't that clever?' she asked admiringly, her face upturned to match the sky.

'Isn't what clever?'

'How it always knows when it's four o'clock, of course.' Then she gave him a wide happy grin when he burst out laughing.

'Walked right into that one, didn't I? Come along, wretch, it seems to have stopped.'

They changed in their rooms and met again by the empty pool. Bryony had pulled a shirt on over her bikini, and was sitting beneath a large striped umbrella, her sketchpad on her knee, when Dries joined her.

'Not coming in?' he asked quietly from behind her.

Squinting up at him, she felt her heart give an odd little trip at the sight of his tanned chest a few inches away from her eyes. 'In a minute,' she mumbled breathlessly.

'All right.' Tossing his towel on the opposite lounger, he turned and dived cleanly into the pool.

This was getting ridiculous. She didn't want to be

aware of him. Dear God, hadn't she been hurt enough in the past? You'd think her stupid body would have more sense than to be attracted to someone again! With a cross little noise in the back of her throat, she slammed her pad down on the tiles and got to her feet. Stripping off her shirt, she sat gingerly on the edge of the pool, her feet in the water, before slowly immersing herself.

She wasn't a very good swimmer, but she thought she might manage to get across the width, and maybe the exercise would dispel thoughts of Dries and the trembling excitement he kept generating. Turning on to her back, she stared up at the impossibly blue sky. It was so hard to believe that she was in Malaysia. Everything had changed so quickly—thrust into close proximity with a wickedly attractive man, a man who would keep teasing her; a brother who kept cleverly managing to be one step ahead of them all the time, and if she hadn't known better, she'd have thought he was doing it on purpose.

Turning over on to her front, she began swimming again. The water was warm, silky, and quite delicious, and slowly, perhaps because of the soft, balmy air, the delicious scents that filled the garden, she relaxed, pushed her odd jumbled thoughts away. Reaching the side, she turned over again and pushed off from the edge, then just let herself float, allowing her mind to drift pleasurably. Clare was safe, there would only be a few more hours to spend in Dries's company—she could cope with that, couldn't she? Of course she could. She should relax, enjoy herself, make the most of this unexpected holiday——Then she let out a squeal of alarm as strong arms encircled her and lifted her clear of the water.

'No! Put me down!' she yelled—so he did, but not quite in the way she expected; for which she had already braced herself, imagining instant immersion. He let go her legs, then slowly lowered her down his own sturdy length until he held her clasped to him, her head on a level with his own, her feet clear of the bottom, and her stomach slid somewhere down by her knees. With his hair slicked back, his lashes sparkling with water, Dries looked like a seal—a very smug seal, Bryony thought, her eyes wide with sudden apprehension. The blue eyes gleamed more brightly for a moment before they moved to her mouth, and warmth coursed through her, tingling her toes.

'I keep getting this quite overwhelming desire to kiss you . . .' he said softly.

'No!' she protested in alarm. 'You mustn't!'

'Why?' he asked humorously. 'Because I don't have dark hair?'

'What? Oh, yes,' she agreed thankfully, grasping at any straw.

'Liar,' he mocked lazily.

'I am not lying! And will you please let me go?' When he didn't comply, she pursed her lips and fought to keep her breathing steady. It would be a fine thing, wouldn't it, if he discovered how he could affect her without even trying? With his sense of humour, heaven knew what would happen. He'd probably take great delight in teasing her just for the hell of it. 'Why are you doing this?' she asked as reasonably as she knew how, determined not to go over the top, over-react. 'In a few hours we'll be going home, we won't see each other again.'

'Won't we?'

'Of course we won't!' Searching his mocking eyes,

she reproved quietly, 'You mustn't flirt with me, Dries, it isn't fair.'

'Isn't it?' he asked smoothly as he trailed his knuckles seductively down her cheek. 'But then who wants to be fair in such beautiful surroundings? A warm sun, a scented garden, and a beautiful woman. What more could a man want?'

'I don't know,' she denied, deliberately obtuse.

'Don't you, Bryony? Bryony with the laughing eyes? Not even one little kiss?'

'No.'

'Why?'

'Because I know just where one little kiss is likely to lead!' she retorted. 'I might look and act like a fool, but, believe me, beneath this daffy exterior is a very hard head.'

'And heart?' he queried.

'And heart,' she confirmed. She'd learned the hard way that a hard heart was much the best answer to everything, and she wasn't about to unlearn all her lessons now. Looking away from him, she stared out over the garden, her expression distant.

'Been hurt, Bryony?' asked Dries softly.

'Yes,' she admitted honestly.

'And it still hurts?'

'No!' she exclaimed unthinkingly, then pulled an exasperated face. She should have said yes.

'Then why?'

'Because I remembered what happened! How much it hurt! Oh, Dries,' she begged unhappily, 'please don't do this. If I let you kiss me, I'll end up liking you more than I want to . . .'

'And that's not allowed? I'm quite a likeable fellow.'

'I know. That's the trouble, but as long as you don't kiss me——'

'You can pretend it wouldn't be a problem. Which it would if I kissed you.'

'Yes.' she admitted, knowing it was true. Every minute in his company deepened the attraction she felt. Kissing him would make everything so much harder to cope with.

'Does everything have to have a deeper meaning with you, Bryony?' he asked quietly. 'No light-hearted flirtations?'

'Oh, yes, sometimes, but only if . . . That's not fair, Dries!' she protested.

'Only if it isn't likely to mean anything?' he persisted. 'And kissing me might mean something?'

'All right—yes!' she burst out in exasperation. 'Now can we drop the subject?'

Staring at her for long moments, he suddenly nodded. Then, releasing her, he swam away.

Surprised, and perhaps a little chagrined that it had meant so little to him after all, Bryony turned and swam back to the side of the pool. Grabbing her towel, she quickly rubbed herself as dry as she could before putting her shirt back on. Sitting on the lounger, she picked up her sketchpad. She was shaking, she found, and her vision had a deplorable tendency to blur. Lying back, she closed her eyes, her sketchpad clutched to her chest like a shield. No regrets, she told herself forcefully. Be sensible—yes. Dries probably thought she was neurotic, which she probably was, but she couldn't, wouldn't, lay herself open to any more hurt.

'There's absolutely no need to look as though you're protecting your honour from the marauding hordes,' he derided as he came to drip beside her.

'I wasn't doing anything of the sort,' she denied stiffly, refusing to look at him. 'I think I'll go and have a shower and change.' Jumping to her feet, she rushed away and into the hotel. She knew he was standing watching her, probably laughing at her, thinking her stupid, and perhaps she was, but it still made her want to cry, because she liked him, and she had *wanted* him to kiss her.

CHAPTER FOUR

BY THE time she had showered and changed, and given herself a very stern talking to, Bryony had herself more or less under control. Wearing the other dress she'd bought in Bangkok, also creased, she went to sit on the empty shaded terrace. She would be cool and polite, she promised herself, aloofly friendly; that was the way to behave. And to make sure her thoughts remained away from Dries, she would do some sketching.

Making sure the pool area really was unoccupied, and that Dries wasn't lurking anywhere, she opened her large sketchbook on her knee. As she gazed round her, searching for inspiration, her eyes settled on a possible subject. With a little nod she began to draw, trying to capture the sheer lassitude of the Malay gardener who was leaning on his hoe gazing into space. He looked incredibly old, his face wrinkled and burnt almost black by the sun, yet there was humour in that lined face, a timelessness, as though he couldn't understand why people rushed around so busily. The world would be there tomorrow—and so it would, Bryony thought with a smile.

Totally absorbed in what she was doing, she was taken by surprise when a Malay waiter came to stand beside her. With a rather startled look, she accepted the coconut with a straw he presented her with.

'Thank you,' she said.

When he remained, clearly curious, she smiled and

gestured for him to stand back a few paces. Turning to a clean page, she swiftly drew his likeness, then, tearing off the sheet, she handed it to him. With a beaming smile he stared wonderingly at his likeness before holding it to his chest as though it were his most prized possession. Then, with another smile, he turned and went back into the hotel.

'You make it look so easy,' Dries murmured from behind her.

'And so it is, for me,' she admitted on a soft indrawn breath. Then, remembering her decision, she deliberately turned to look up at him. He looked much as he normally did, no hint of mockery in his level gaze, and she relaxed slightly. 'Nothing I can take any great credit for,' she explained evenly. 'It's a gift I was born with.'

'And one you've perfected,' he added, coming to sit opposite her. 'What are you drinking?' he asked, eyeing the coconut.

'I haven't the faintest idea,' she confessed with a little grin, entirely forgetting the aloof, friendly bit, and anyway quite incapable of being anything but herself. 'The waiter brought it, asked me something I didn't understand, and he looked so hopeful that I said yes.'

Shaking his head at her, Dries waited until the waiter returned before ordering a gin and tonic. 'What else were you drawing?' he asked.

'The gardener, but I couldn't get it right.' Tearing off the page, she went to crumple it, only Dries stopped her. Taking it out of her hand, he stared down at it.

'What's wrong with it?' he queried. 'It looks perfect to me.'

'But not to me.' Giving him a warm smile, because—well, because she liked him and he had obviously understood her behaviour earlier and wasn't going to be difficult, Bryony consciously registered his appearance for the first time. His strong jaw was freshly shaved, his hair freshly washed, and the blue shirt he was wearing made his eyes look brighter. 'You look nice,' she approved artlessly, as she returned her attention to her pad. 'You should always wear blue.'

Unaware of the gentle amusement with which he was regarding her, she propped her feet on the rung of his chair and began sketching again, her attention focused solely on what she was doing. It took four attempts before she was satisfied. Staring from her drawing to the gardener and back again, she gave a little nod of approval. She would keep this one, and if she could reproduce it in clay, she might get it cast in bronze. It was damned expensive, but what the hell?

'May I see?' Dries asked softly.

'Sure.' Turning the pad round, she showed him, and, taking it from her, he stared down at it thoughtfully for some time before handing it back.

'Will you sculpt it?' he asked.

'Yes, I think I might. It—pleases me,' Bryony admitted almost cautiously. 'Don't you find it extraordinary that everyone's face is so different?' she went on. 'I mean, there can only be a certain number of noses, shape of eye, mouth, and yet no two faces are ever alike. Extraordinary.'

'Yet they say that each of us has a double, don't they?'

'Oh, they, they,' she said on a laugh. 'Who are they?

And I've never seen any doubles, and I constantly examine faces.'

'Is that what you do best?' he asked interestedly.

'Mm. I like faces!' she exclaimed, and he laughed.

'What will you do with the rejects? Keep them?'

'Heavens, no! They aren't any good.'

'May I have them?' Dries asked.

'No,' she refused bluntly, and when he looked amazed, she explained, 'They're imperfect.' Before he could stop her she tore them in half and put them on the table. 'Call it vanity,' she said softly with a small conciliatory smile, and, because she was grateful that he had made her feel comfortable again, she took her pad back and began sketching him instead. With her head tilted to one side, her lip once again caught between her teeth, she added the finishing touches before turning it to show him.

'Oh, Bryony!' he exclaimed softly, his eyes full of laughter. 'The Lord High Executioner? A laughing executioner at that! Is that really how you see me?'

'No, of course not.' Taking the pad from him and tearing off the page, she thought for a moment, then with a teasing little smile she began again, this time drawing him as a medieval knight, his hair slightly longer, chain mail and armour encasing his splendid body, a plumed helmet beneath his arm.

He sat looking at it for a long time after she had handed him the pad. 'Quite amazing,' he said softly. 'Quite utterly amazing.' Then with a rather endearingly crooked smile, he confessed, 'I don't know what to say. But you're not having this one to tear up!'

'All right,' she agreed warmly.

'Thank you, I shall treasure it,' he promised with a courtly little bow, or as courtly as he could manage sitting down.

'You're welcome.' Picking up her drink, Bryony then nearly threw it all over herself as a loud voice exclaimed in astonishment from somewhere behind her.

'Brains!'

Turning round, she stared, then smiled as her brother hurried towards her. 'Good grief, you look like a hippy!' she reproved, getting to her feet. Grinning, nearly knocking over her chair in her haste to get to him, she grabbed his bony shoulders and shook him, then gave him a big hug. 'Wretch! Utter wretch!'

'Me?' Daniel exclaimed, not looking terribly pleased to see her. 'What have I done? And what on earth are you doing here?'

'I came with Dries, of course. Clare's uncle,' Bryony clarified as he looked puzzled.

'Why?' he asked bluntly. 'Well, go on, why did you? A year,' he added bitterly, 'that's all I asked. One lousy year away, and what do I get? A besotted teenager turning up in Hong Kong declaring undying affection! Cryptic messages left all over the place from her uncle; Clare behaving as though the end of the world had come! And now you turning up! For God's sake, Bryony, I'm not a child! I agreed to ring you each week, wasn't that enough?'

'It wasn't me!' she retorted, incensed, when she was finally able to get a word in edgeways 'And I've never treated you like a child!' she denied strongly. 'And if you'd stuck to your itinerary, none of this would have happened anyway! We've been chasing you all over the place!'

'Well, I didn't ask you to!' snapped Daniel.

'I didn't say you did! And please stop shouting at

me! Oh, look, this is ridiculous.' Mortified, bitterly aware of Dries's being an interested bystander, Bryony turned to indicate him. 'This is Clare's uncle——'

'So?' Daniel interrupted rudely.

'So he's come to take Clare home! She never told him she was coming; he thought she was still in school.'

'Well, that doesn't surprise me!' he bit out. 'She's the most spoilt, petulant little brat it's ever been my misfortune to meet! And I'm telling you, B——'

'Where is she?' Dries put in quietly, getting to his feet and coming to stand beside them.

'Oh, ask me another!' Daniel burst out aggrievedly.

'I don't want to know another,' Dries denied in the same hatefully controlled voice that was guaranteed to put up the back of a saint, let alone Daniel, 'I want to know this one. Where is she?'

Staring at Dries, a look of bored insolence on his face that made Bryony's heart sink further, Daniel said slowly, 'I haven't the faintest idea. She is not, thank heavens, my responsibility.' With a nasty little smile that made Bryony cringe, he turned away.

With a little smile that was even nastier, Dries grabbed his arm and swung him back, 'Don't,' he said softly, 'turn your back on me when I'm talking to you. Clare is seventeen years old. You, however unwillingly, assumed responsibility for her when you invited her out here. Now, where—is—she?' he grated.

'Invite her? Are you kidding?' jeered Daniel. 'The only thing I'd invite her to do is throw herself off the nearest cliff! And take your damned hand off my arm!'

His eyes glacial, his face set hard, Dries slowly increased the pressure and began forcing Daniel along the terrace.

'No!' screamed Bryony, chasing after them. 'Dries, you let him go!'

'Shut up, Bryony,' Dries said savagely as he continued to force Daniel round the side of the hotel and out of sight of the few people who had wandered out on to the terrace.

Grabbing Dries's hand, she tried to force his fingers away from her brother's arm. 'Stop it, Dries! You're just making things worse! Let him go, damn you!'

'Very well,' he bit out, giving her a look of hatred. Releasing Daniel, he leaned back against the hotel wall, arms folded across his chest, and stared at the younger man. 'Now, where is my niece?'

Bryony, staring from one to the other, from Dries's intolerance to Daniel's cynicism, temper darkening his brown eyes, felt sick. Was this the real Dries? she wondered. This hard-eyed stranger? Was this the man who had amassed a fortune? The man who pursued an exacting profession? Because, despite his light-hearted description of his work, it was exacting, she knew, and to be the best in the business he had to be more than an amiable giant, didn't he? He had to be ruthless. He looked ruthless now, and she was suddenly frightened for Daniel, who would be incapable of realising the danger of provoking him. Daniel's cynicism was only a mask to hide his inadequacies, or what he thought of as his inadequacies, but Dries wouldn't realise that.

'Daniel,' she whispered warningly, 'please tell him where she is.'

'Why the hell should I?' snapped her brother.

'Because, whatever you might think of her, she's only seventeen, and Dries is worried about her.'

With a little shrug that made her want to hit him, he drawled, 'Singapore.'

'Singapore?' Bryony exclaimed in disbelief. 'What the hell is she doing in Singapore?'

'Search me.'

Feeling, more than seeing, the move Dries made, she placed herself between the two of them and pleaded frantically, 'Daniel, please!'

Throwing Dries a glance of derision, he drawled slowly, 'I need a drink.' Without looking at his sister, he walked back round to the terrace and sat down.

'Nice, did you say?' Dries asked coldly.

'He *is* nice!' Bryony retorted furiously, near to tears. 'You shouldn't have put his back up!'

'Oh, I'm so sorry.' With a look every bit as derisory as Daniel's, Dries to walked back to the terrace.

Collapsing weakly back against the wall, she closed her eyes, Oh, God. What on earth was Clare doing in Singapore? With a long, shaky sigh, she pushed her untidy hair off her forehead. She wanted to run away, hide . . .

'Bryony.' Dries's voice wasn't raised, but it carried very effectively and it would have taken more than her small store of courage to ignore it. With an unhappy little sigh, she went to join him and Daniel.

At least they were no longer shouting at each other, she saw as she hovered at the corner. Dries was leaning forward, talking urgently: Daniel was looking mutinous. Oh, why couldn't he just tell him? Why did he have to be so contrary all the time? And why on earth had she ever come here? If she hadn't come, she wouldn't have been involved, wouldn't have known about this confrontation would have been comfortable. Forcing herself to move forward before she provoked another row, she took a chair beside her brother.

'I'll see if I can get a flight,' Dries said wearily, getting to his feet and going inside the hotel.

'Why did she go to Singapore?' Bryony asked her brother urgently.

'I just told him.'

'Well, now you can tell me!' she yelled, her voice wavering out of control.

'Keep your voice down!' he hissed, then with a long sigh he said grudgingly, 'We had a row—another one,' he added disgustedly, 'so she went off to Singapore with some of the students she met in Bangkok.'

'When did she go? asked Bryony.

'Yesterday, after she got her uncle's note. I told her to stay put, but she refused.'

'Well, why on earth didn't you stop her?'

'Why the hell should I?' he demanded. 'I'm not her keeper! And how the devil was I to know she was out here without permission?'

Staring at him, Bryony suddenly remembered that Dries had said the hotel had said Clare was still there. Frowning, she asked, 'But why didn't the hotel know she'd gone? When we asked this morning . . .'

With an irritable movement, Daniel shoved his hand in his pocket, drew out an envelope and tossed it on the table in front of her. 'They didn't know. I found that shoved under my door after she'd gone. A note and some money to pay her hotel bill.'

'Oh, Daniel, what a mess!' she sighed.

'You can say that again. I'm sick to death of altering, then re-altering my damned arrangements. I had this all worked out down to the last half-hour, and now look at me!'

'I'm sorry,' she said lamely.

'So I should bloody well think! And what the hell did you have to go and tell *him*for?' demanded Daniel.

'Because I thought he should know. How was I supposed to know she'd gone without telling anyone? Oh, Daniel, please stop being difficult,' she pleaded. 'It's bad enough without your putting Dries's back up further.'

'I didn't put his back up further! He damned well assumed I was in the wrong! Oh, all right,' he capitulated grudgingly. 'Sorry, Brains. Only there was no need for him to treat me as though I were a white slaver! And I'm damned if I can understand why you came,' he added. 'You're hopeless at this sort of thing. Look at you—one row, and you fall apart at the seams!'

'I know,' she admitted miserably, 'and it wasn't my idea to come.'

'It was mine,' Dries admitted returning to sit in his chair. 'I've booked us on the nine-thirty flight in the morning. There isn't an earlier one.'

'Do we know which hotel she's in?' Bryony asked drearily, wondering if she dared suggest she go home. Back to England. He didn't really need her any more.

'Not the name. Your brother is returning to his hotel later to find someone who does.'

'A couple of students didn't go with them,' Daniel explained. 'They'll know.'

'Can't you ask them now?' said Dries.

'No, I can't ask them now! They've gone on a trip round the island and won't be back until late.' Staring at Dries, defiance in every line of him, Daniel asked insolently, 'Are we eating here?'

'We can do,' Dries agreed coldly. Turning in his chair, he beckoned the waiter and asked if there was a table for three.

'Most certainly, sir,' the waiter said, bowing, a wide smile on his face. Obviously relieved they hadn't come to blows, Bryony thought half hysterically. 'If you will come this way?'

Getting to their feet, they all trailed into the restaurant, with Daniel and Dries metaphorically circling each other like pit bull terriers about to fight.

When they were seated, the air practically thick enough to cut with a knife, Dries eyed Daniel disdainfully, then with the obvious intention of striving for some sort of normality, or as near normality as they were likely to get, he asked coolly, 'Why did you call your sister Brains? Because she doesn't have any?'

'No, because she does,' Daniel replied with the same flat inflexion Dries was using. 'If you ever want to know the answer to anything, just ask Bryony. She always knows the answer.'

'Not always,' she demurred, wishing teleportation were a viable proposition.

'Nearly always. You didn't get to St Andrews by using your smile!'

'St Andrews University?' Dries asked with unflattering disbelief, 'In Scotland?'

'Yes. She got a first—and they don't give those out like paper hankies!' exclaimed Daniel, his anger for the moment overcome by his desire to boast, and Bryony gave him a faint smile, rather touched by his championship.

'No, they don't,' Dries agreed, staring at Bryony with fresh interest. 'What did you read?'

'Fine Arts. Oxford didn't have a course that year . . .'

'But Oxford would have accepted you?'

'Yes.'

'Good Lord!' Shaking his head, Dries turned back to Daniel, and, holding the younger man's eyes for long moments, he finally continued, 'All right, now that we've both calmed down, perhaps you'd explain about Clare. You said she just turned up in Hong Kong.'

'Yes,' he confirmed, his head tilted in a defiant attitude that Bryony knew only too well. 'I dare say I was partly to blame,' he admitted magnanimously. 'I seem to remember I waxed rather enthusiastic about it when we met in Paris. It never occurred to me why she might want to know my exact itinerary, dates and places.' Taking a mouthful of the wine that Dries had ordered, he stared down into his glass as though searching for inspiration. 'Anyway, as I said, she just turned up. She tagged along, getting more and more dissatisfied because she wanted to go to all the places I didn't . . .'

'Such as?'

'Exotic night spots.' Daniel stated, throwing down another mental gauntlet. When Dries refused to pick it up, he shrugged and resumed, 'She perked up a bit in Bangkok, after we'd changed to a swanky hotel, that is, and she could lord it over everybody. Only then she got talking to some students who persisted in extolling the virtues of Penang, and—well, I was coming here anyway, so I agreed. It's usually less wearing on the nerves to give in to Clare than argue with her.'

'And at least you didn't just dump her, leave her to fend for herself,' Bryony put in, hoping to smooth things even further. 'That was kind of you.'

'Go on,' said Dries, not looking in the least grateful for Bryony's assistance or Daniel's supposed chivalry.

'When we got here to Georgetown, and she found that message from you telling her to stay put . . . Well, that was a damned stupid thing to do,' Daniel denigrated forcefully. 'You should have just turned up! Giving Clare warnings is fatal! The next thing I knew, she'd upped sticks and shoved off! If I'd known she was out here without your knowledge, I'd have been more suspicious of her behaviour. Only I didn't! I thought you were just playing the heavy uncle, checking up on her . . .'

'And, having no doubt suffered a similar fate from your sister, you had every sympathy for her predicament,' Dries put in pithily. Lowering his eyes, he twisted his wine glass round and round, his face distant as though he had now opted out of the proceedings.

'Something like that,' Daniel agreed bluntly. Turning his shoulder on Dries, he stared critically at Bryony. 'You're too thin,' he reproved. 'I bet you haven't been eating again.'

'Yes, I have,' she declared.

'Huh, not much, by the look of you. Did you finish those chess pieces?'

'Chess pieces?' queried Dries, startled out of his preoccupation.

'Yes, chess pieces. You don't need to sound so incredulous,' Daniel sneered. 'They were commissioned by Sir Edward March.'

'The actor?'

'Yes. He saw the set she'd carved for Viscount Emmerson, little caricatures of his immediate family, and rang her the next day demanding a set of his own depicting famous actors and actresses.'

'My, my, you do move in influential circles!' Dries commented, sounding horribly sarcastic. 'And each piece was carved to represent a member of his family?'

'Yes,' Daniel answered for her, 'the pawns his children, the rook his uncle and so on. She did them from a set of photographs, didn't you?'

'Yes,' Bryony admitted quietly, refusing to look at either of them. She knew what was Daniel was doing—he always did it. She didn't know why; it was as though he gained some sort of comfort by boasting about her achievements. Perhaps it was the only thing about her that he admired. Only she wished he hadn't told Dries about her; it made her feel uncomfortable. She would much rather he'd gone on thinking her daffy. Then she wondered why. What possible difference could it make now? Was it embarrassment? Yes, perhaps that was it. Never very happy talking about herself, she much preferred people to think her an amiable fool. People expected things of you if you were clever, expected you to behave in a certain way. The way Sir Edward March had expected her to behave, she thought with a sigh, after someone had told him of her education. He had expected long, erudite discussions on the whys and wherefores of carving—method, execution, careful choice of material, and had seemed bewildered when she'd told him she used whatever happened to feel right at the time. 'He seemed quite pleased, though,' she added distantly, as though no time had elapsed since the question had been asked before giving her answer.

'Pleased? Yes, I should think he was,' Dries commented. 'I've been in serious danger of underestimating you, haven't I?'

'Everyone does,' said Daniel, as though the thought gave him enormous pleasure, and Bryony gave him a faint bewildered smile.

'Do you want me to book you a room here for the night?' Dries asked, 'or will you stay at your own hotel and meet us at the airport in the morning?'

'Why should I want to meet you at the airport in the morning?' Daniel asked in astonishment.

'Because we're flying to Singapore,' Dries said neutrally.

'So? I don't need to see you off, do I?'

'No, Daniel, you need to be on the flight with us.'

'Oh, no,' he denied, throwing up his hands, 'no way! I'm getting on with my holiday.'

'Daniel,' Dries said very quietly, his blue eyes hard and steady, and looking suddenly very, very dangerous, 'you are coming to Singapore.'

'I'm bloody not! Just because you're the most sought-after special effects man in the business and no doubt used to giving orders, don't think you can order me about! I'm not one of your minions, and I have absolutely no intention of hanging on your coat tails, whether you expect it or not!'

'I'm not asking you to hang on my coat tails, I'm telling you that you're coming to Singapore!' Slapping his hands flat on the table as though about to get up and storm out, Dries grabbed the front of Daniel's T-shirt and held him still.

Unable to take any more, Bryony slipped from her chair with a little cry of distress and ran out.

'Now look what you've done!' Daniel exclaimed. Wrenching his shirt out of Dries's fist, he lurched upright and followed his sister.

'Oh, damn it!' Dries said wearily. Throwing his napkin down in disgust, he got to his feet.

Gaining the comparative sanctuary of the sea wall, Bryony clutched at a nearby palm and stared out over the Straits. Her vision blurred, she blinked rapidly, then stiffened and tried to shrug away when Daniel grasped her shoulders and turned her round.

'Now calm down,' he said gruffly, giving her a little shake. 'We were only arguing, nothing to get het up about.'

'I feel sick,' she muttered shakily.

'I know, I'm sorry—but honestly, Brains, he's so bloody arrogant!'

'No, he isn't,' she denied quietly, 'not really. Oh, Daniel, why couldn't you have explained things to him reasonably instead of losing your temper?' she wailed. 'You know I can't cope with rows and arguments.'

'I know,' he muttered awkwardly, kicking irritably at the sea wall. 'He put my back up. And why the hell is it so important that I come to Singapore?'

'Because he doesn't know what Clare looks like.' Then Bryony listlessly explained the reasons Dries had given her.

'Well, why the hell didn't he say so? Honestly! All right, all right I'll come to bloody Singapore,' Daniel added peevishly. 'Boy, ever since that little bitch turned up I haven't had a minute's peace!' Catching sight of Dries standing a few feet away, he turned and gave him a bitter glance. 'What time does this plane go, then?'

'Nine-thirty.'

'Right, I'll meet you at the airport at nine o'clock!' Returning his attention to Bryony, he stooped and pressed an awkward kiss on her forehead. 'I'll see you in the morning. And for God's sake stop worrying!' Turning on his heel, he strode off.

'Are you all right?' Dries asked quietly, coming to stand beside her.

'Yes.'

'I suppose you want me to apologise,' he continued.

'No.'

'No,' he echoed on a funny little sigh. 'Back to being a mouse, are we? A monosyllabic one at that.'

'Well, what did you expect?' Bryony asked miserably. 'I told you and told you I couldn't cope with rows and arguments, and what do you do? Pick a quarrel with him.'

'Well, he was hardly all sweetness and light, was he?' Dries asked disgruntledly. 'I don't think I've ever met a more difficult, bloody-minded——'

'He isn't,' she denied stonily.

'Bryony . . .'

'Well, only when people accuse him of things he hasn't done,' she qualified.

'I didn't accuse him of anything! I merely asked where Clare was!'

'It wasn't what you asked him, it was the way you asked him. I think I'll go home,' she added unhappily. 'You don't need me in Singapore.'

'Yes, I do,' Dries said gently, moving to turn her to

face him, 'even if only as mediator. Only one more day—you can cope with that, can't you?'

'And supposing it isn't one more day? Supposing when we get to Singapore Clare's flown again?'

'Then I'll let you go back to England and I'll fly after her—dragging your brother with me, of course.'

'Oh, Dries!' Letting her breath out on a tired sigh, Bryony leaned her forehead against his strong chest. 'I can't help being such a little coward.'

'I know,' he sympathised, holding her close, then he leant his head on top of hers in a comforting gesture. 'You're shaking.'

'Yes.' Sliding her arms around him, Bryony turned her head so that her cheek lay against his heart and the gentle rhythm seemed very reassuring. 'When I was a little girl, my parents used to fight all the time. They always sounded so bitter, so acrimonious, as though they really hated each other. I used to hide in the broom cupboard, my hands over my ears, and always, always, afterwards, I used to be sick.'

'Poor Bryony,' Dries said softly. 'Didn't they fight when you were a big girl?'

'What?' she asked, puzzled, raising her head to look at him.

With a half-smile, he explained, 'You said when you were little, as though the fighting stopped when you grew up.'

'Oh, no, I expect they still fought. I wasn't there when I grew up. Daniel isn't a bad person, Dries,' she added entreatingly, 'truly he isn't, and what he told you was the truth. I know it seems as though I didn't bring him up very well, and perhaps I didn't, but he isn't a bad person. Selfish perhaps, but then I'm selfish—I suspect most people are. He just doesn't like being accused of things—well, nobody does, do they?'

'No, all right, I'll suspend judgement until I've talked to Clare. Does that make you feel better?'

'Not really, because you sound as though you know what the judgement will be,' she explained.

'Then can't we agree to differ? I don't want to argue with you, upset you any more, and obviously you know him better than I do.'

'Well, I thought I did,' she sighed. 'He seemed to think . . .'

'That you were over-protective?' he asked, his voice gentle, kind.

'Yes.' Leaning her head back against him, she inhaled deeply. The scents seemed stronger now that darkness had fallen. It had been light when she had run from the restaurant, and now suddenly it was dark. She had read about night falling swiftly, without the transitory period that they had in England, but she had never experienced it until now. The cicadas had begun their nightly chorus too, and she listened to them as she slowly relaxed against Dries's strong frame. The moon hung like a big silver ball in the dark velvet sky, stars that seemed so much closer than at home. Lights twinkled far out in the Straits, fishing-boats perhaps, or a pleasure cruise. When Dries touched gentle fingers to her hair she closed her eyes with a little sigh that was almost contentment.

'Feeling better now?' he asked.

'Yes, thank you,' she said in a polite, little-girl voice that made him smile.

'Good. You smell of sunshine,' he observed, his

voice slightly husky.

'Do I?' she asked absently, moving slightly so that she could look up into his face. Humour lurked in his eyes, and his mouth was quirked in a smile as he shifted to lean against the wall and draw her between his powerful thighs so that her face was on a level with his own—and suddenly his expression changed, grew serious, and tension crackled between them. With a sharp indrawn breath, Bryony tried to move away.

'Ah, no, stay,' he said softly, 'Just for a while, to relax, unwind. If you go in now, you won't sleep, will you? You'll worry all round the subject until you make yourself ill again.'

Not sure that that was entirely true, she nevertheless halted. It would look silly if she rushed away—and he was only being kind, not . . . Her eyes fixed widely on his, a rather haunted expression in their soft depths, she began to chew uncertainly on her lower lip.

'Don't,' he reproved, his voice husky, his eyes on her mouth. Lifting his hand, he gently eased her lip free with his finger. 'You'll make it sore.'

Her insides fluttery, like a million butterflies unable to settle, Bryony felt her breath jerk in her throat at his touch. 'I——' she began.

'I think you're standing too far away,' he continued, his voice low, barely audible. Linking his arms loosely round her, he examined her exquisite face until she wriggled in embarrassment.

'Don't,' she commanded shakily, her voice slightly thick. 'You promised, Dries . . .'

'No, I didn't—and oh, Bryony,' he sighed, 'I do so yearn to kiss you. I've been wanting it all day. Close your eyes,' he persuaded softly.

'No,' she groaned. 'Please, Dries!'

'If we go home tomorrow, you'll never ever know what you've missed.'

'I don't want to know what I've missed. I told you——' then she felt her heart jerk in surprise as he caught her tight against him and parted her mouth, his tongue sliding sweetly inside before she had a chance to deny him.

Stiffening, she tried to jerk free, then moaned deep in her throat when he wouldn't release her, but continued his assault, however gently it was made. Frightened of the way he could so easily make her feel, she pushed against his shoulders, and when that failed, in desperation and panic, knowing that if she didn't break free soon she would respond, she grasped a handful of his hair and pulled. When he gasped and released her, she took off, running as hard as she could towards the hotel.

Dries caught her as she reached the wall where flowers rioted in scented profusion. Dragging her to a halt, he turned her and pushed her back against the laden boughs, releasing the sweet, heavy perfume.

'No,' she pleaded. 'Please—no, Dries!'

Ignoring her, he crushed her shaking body against him and bent his head to expertly capture her aching mouth. With a little sob, Bryony abandoned her futile struggle with her common sense and clenched her fingers against his broad back, because she wanted so much to kiss, and be kissed by him. Just once.

'Your tongue,' he breathed against her mouth. 'Use your tongue.'

Her body liquefying, knowing she should draw back, only suddenly, almost desperately, not wanting to, wanting, for the first time in their acquaintance, to know the ultimate pleasure that this man could bring, she pushed her tongue against his, then into his mouth. As his body arched slowly against hers, she pressed closer, held him, kissed him with a need she had tried too long to deny, and two years of repressed feelings exploded into life, shattering her control. There was no space anywhere between them; his thighs were pressed hard against hers, trapping her, his stomach flat against her ribs, his powerful chest crushing her breasts. When his mouth shifted, moved, pressed softly, hard, then soft again, she shuddered, then dragged a deep sobbing breath into her lungs as his teeth nipped gently at her tongue, tasted the inner surfaces of her lips.

It was madness, she knew it was, but she seemed unable to stop. She didn't want to stop, because it was beautiful and exciting, like being in a warm, special dream where nothing intruded except the feel of Dries's hard, aroused body pressed to hers, the scent on the breeze, the muted sound of the cicadas, and their breath that mingled as lungs fought to drag air into them and then expel it.

Her hair had long since come loose and the gentle breeze blew it softly round her face as Dries moved fractionally, allowed her to withdraw, breathe more easily. Lifting lids that felt far too heavy, she stared bemusedly into his deep blue eyes, eyes that looked as drugged as hers felt.

'Oh, God,' she whispered.

'Yes,' he agreed thickly, bending to capture her mouth once more, one large warm palm moving to cup her breast.

'No,' she denied hoarsely, dragging herself free. 'No!' Unable to look at him, knowing guiltily that she

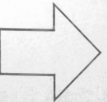

NO COST! NO OBLIGATION TO BUY!
NO PURCHASE NECESSARY!

PLAY "LUCKY 7"
AND GET AS MANY AS SIX FREE GIFTS...

HOW TO PLAY:

1. With a coin, carefully scratch off the silver box at the right. This makes you eligible to receive one or more free books, and possibly other gifts, depending on what is revealed beneath the scratch-off area.

2. You'll receive brand-new Harlequin Presents® novels. When you return this card, we'll send you the books and gifts you qualify for *absolutely* free!

3. If we don't hear from you, every month we'll send you 6 additional novels to read and enjoy. You can return them and owe nothing but if you want to keep them, they are yours at the specially discounted subscribers price of only $2.22 each plus 25¢ delivery and applicable sales tax, if any*. That's the complete price, and—compared to cover prices of $2.75 each in stores—quite a bargain!

4. When you join the Harlequin Reader Service®, you'll get our monthly newsletter as well as additional free gifts from time to time just for being a subscriber.

5. You must be completely satisfied. You may cancel at any time simply by sending us a note or a shipping statement marked ''cancel'' or returning any shipment to us at our cost.

DETACH AND MAIL CARD TODAY

BUSINESS REPLY MAIL

FIRST CLASS MAIL   PERMIT NO. 717   BUFFALO, NY

POSTAGE WILL BE PAID BY ADDRESSEE

HARLEQUIN READER SERVICE
3010 WALDEN AVE
PO BOX 1867
BUFFALO NY 14240-9952

NO POSTAGE
NECESSARY
IF MAILED
IN THE
UNITED STATES

shouldn't have let things get so out of control, she leaned her head back against the wall and closed her eyes. Confused, uncertain, aching, she fought to steady her breathing. She couldn't believe she had responded like that, and, now that her senses were returning, she felt ashamed. She could have stopped him, had she really wanted to. Lifting weighted lids, she stared at him numbly. 'I——' she began.

'Don't!' he warned, his own breathing ragged and uncontrolled. 'Don't tell me this is not to happen again; or that you won't have an affair with me, or indeed even a light flirtation. Don't tell me you're going to be sensible, and strong; don't tell me anything at all—your response said it all for you. No . . .' he repeated, putting a hand across her mouth when she opened it to protest.

Staring at him, Bryony grasped his hand and moved it aside, 'But I am going to tell you that. I——'

'No more games, Bryony.'

'I'm not playing games,' she protested weakly.

'Aren't you?' he asked, his voice still slightly thick.

'No.'

Placing a hand on each side of her, Dries stared down into the pale oval of her face. 'You knew how you made me feel. Knew that I wanted to make love to you, to hold your naked body in my arms, taste you, touch you——'

'No,' she whispered, her eyes enormous with entreaty. 'Please, no!' she begged. She hadn't known that.

'Yes. And you want it as much as I do.'

'I don't,' she denied weakly, moving her head agitatedly from side to side, because she knew she did. And there was such a terrible temptation to say yes, to say to hell with tomorrow, to let him love her . . . but if she did that, she would never be able to cope when he left—as leave he would; that was as inevitable as night following day. They always left.

CHAPTER FIVE

'YOU don't need to look so worried,' Dries reproved, a derisive twist to his mouth. 'I'm not about to ravish you!'

'No, I know—I'm sorry, but I couldn't cope if I had an affair with you,' Bryony said achingly, her hands twisted together in front of her. 'I'll go home tomorrow. We won't see each other again, that will be best.'

'Will it? For whom? Oh, go to bed,' he ordered tiredly, 'before this iron control cracks and exposes me for the fraud I really am. I don't even know why I'm persisting,' he added to himself as he urged her towards her room. 'It isn't in the least like me.'

'I'm sorry,' she repeated lamely, not even really sure for what she was apologising.

'Are you? I wonder. You're a dangerous lady, Bryony— I think I knew that the first time I saw you in the garden standing with that little-girl-lost look on your face and a fascinating smile in your eyes. What a pity I didn't realise then that you were going to destroy my peace of mind!'

'But I didn't intend to!' she protested. He made it sound as though it had all been calculated, and it hadn't.

'No, but you say the damnedest things with a look of innocence that's positively lethal. And telling a man he looks nice is tantamount to telling him you find him attractive, and from someone like you that's not at all

99

wise; it gives a man ideas.'

'But I do find you attractive, that's half the trouble,' Bryony exclaimed unhappily, 'although I didn't mean to give you ideas.'

'Didn't you? Wasn't there just a trace of power testing?'

'No!' But was there? she wondered worriedly.

When she looked even more troubled, Dries gave a faint self-mocking smile. With a gentle finger, he touched her nose.

'Don't!' she protested, putting a hand against his chest as though to push him away, then she caught her breath as he covered it with his and held it tight against him.

'Such a little thing, to cause me so much trouble! What am I going to do about you, Bryony Grant?'

'Nothing! You're not to do anything!' she exclaimed with frightened determination, her voice low and urgent. 'You're being deliberately unkind, and it won't do! I've told you and told you I won't have an affair with you, and it's not fair to keep trying to confuse me!'

'I know. The trouble is, I like trying to confuse you—and I don't feel in the least like being fair.'

'But it doesn't mean anything to you!' she wailed.

'Doesn't it?' he asked on a long sigh. 'Would it make any difference if it did?'

'No,' she denied unhappily.

She thought for a moment he wasn't going to leave it there, but finally, with a little shrug that looked irritable rather than accepting, he released her hand and stepped back.

'All right,' he agreed flatly.

Turning her head away so that he wouldn't see the

silly tears that suddenly flooded into her eyes, Bryony
blinked furiously and began to walk towards her room.
Well, what did you expect? she asked herself angrily.
For him to argue with you? Try to persuade you?

She lay awake for a long time in the wide empty bed,
her hands linked beneath her head as she went over
and over all that had happened. She should have felt
relieved, thankful that Dries had accepted her refusal,
only she didn't, she felt confused and lonely and
aching. And her ardent response, instead of cleansing
her, getting it out of her system, only made her want
more.

Why didn't people listen when you told them
things? she wondered despairingly. She'd told him she
didn't want to be kissed—yet did she really wish he
hadn't? No, she thought on a long sigh, she didn't
think she wished that at all. But it had to end here—and
if she hadn't been such a damned little coward she
could have been snuggled up against that warm strong
body, she could have . . . Groaning, she rolled over and
buried her face in the pillow. All he wanted was a
holiday romance, and for her it would have been so
much more, she would have wanted so much more,
and it would have ended in tears and heartache.
Warmth and caring, allowing people to get too close,
was a price too high to pay. When it all went wrong,
as it invariably would, the ache would be so much
more than this. The emptiness she felt now was minor
in comparison to what it would be if she allowed
herself to become too fond of him, and she forcefully
ignored the voice that told her it was too late.

Breakfast was a silent, awkward affair, both of them

preoccupied, and Bryony was glad when it was time to leave for the airport. Daniel was already there when they arrived, and she gave him a faint smile.

'You look terrible,' he pronounced with typical brotherly candour. 'Didn't you sleep?'

'Not much, no,' she confessed, then wondered what he'd say if she told him the reasons hadn't had anything to do with himself or Clare.

'What's up with him?' he asked, indicating Dries, who stood off to one side looking grim. 'You'd think that now he'd got his own way he'd be a bundle of laughs.'

'I don't know,' she sighed, and she didn't, not really. Dries's grim mood might not have anything to do with her at all. Probably didn't, she thought despondently; he'd probably forgotten all about the incident in the garden. 'Did you find out the name of the hotel Clare's gone to?' she asked.

'Yes.'

'Do you think she'll be there?'

'How the hell should I know?' snapped Daniel. Then, presumably realising that wasn't a very helpful thing to say, he comforted, 'Sure she will. I bet we'll walk into the hotel and she'll be the first person we see.'

'That sounds suspiciously like wishful thinking,' Bryony reproved.

'Yeah, I guess it is, but at least then I'll be able to get on with my trip.' As he turned to stare at Dries, an expression of rather wicked glee spread across Daniel's thin face. 'And if he's expecting a meek, biddable teenager, he's in for a shock!'

'Oh, Daniel,' Bryony sighed, 'you're such a comfort to me! Is she really that bad?'

'Worse,' he confirmed, cheering up enormously at the thought of Dries du Vaal's impending discomfort. 'In fact,' he added maliciously, 'I might even stick around for a bit to watch the fireworks.'

'Then you can stick around on your own,' she said shortly. 'I'm going back to England on the first available flight!'

As the tannoy burst into noisy, static life, they picked up their bags and went to join Dries at the departure gate.

When they landed in Singapore, they took a taxi to the hotel, and, leaving Dries to pay it off, Bryony and Daniel walked into reception, and uncannily, true to his prediction, there was Clare. She was standing at the desk wearing the shortest of white shorts and unsuitable high-heeled white shoes, and Bryony blinked in surprise. She had been expecting a sophisticated, worldly-wise young lady, not this girl who seemed younger than her seventeen years. She was having some sort of argument with the clerk, and as Dries joined them Daniel gave a faint smile.

'There, my interfering friend,' he pronounced mockingly, 'is your niece.'

Stealing a glance at Dries's face, Bryony suddenly felt very sorry for him. He looked distinctly reluctant. She wanted to reassure him, she found, only she didn't know how. Apart from which, she thought unhappily, she doubted he'd welcome her interference. Their easy friendship had gone, probably never to be regained.

'Thank you,' muttered Dries before walking across to join Clare, and the deep breath he took was clearly audible.

As Clare turned, Bryony glanced at her brother, a

nasty little doubt lodging in her mind. 'She's beautiful,' she whispered.

'Oh, yes, I never said she wasn't,' he derided.

Turning back to stare at Clare, who was still gazing wide-eyed at Dries, Bryony examined the sweet young face framed by short fair curls. She had the look of a Botticelli angel, the innocence of youth—hardly surprising that Dries had cast Daniel as the baddie. This young lady looked as though butter wouldn't even get in her mouth, let alone melt there. Then, much to Bryony's surprise, she flung herself into Dries's arms and burst into noisy sobs.

It didn't seem to surprise Daniel. 'Par for the course, he muttered cynically.

'What's that supposed to mean?' Bryony asked absently, her eyes on Dries as he tried ineffectually to comfort his niece. 'Should we go and help, do you think?'

'No, I don't. She'll weep only long enough to work out what tale she's going to tell, then the tears will miraculously dry and she'll give him a sweet little-girl smile, Yuk!'

'Daniel!' she reproved, shocked by his bitterness. 'That wasn't very nice.'

'Nice?' her brother exclaimed. 'I thought it was very restrained of me in the circumstances. Er—oh,' he continued as Clare's eyes made brief startled contact with his, 'guess who's going to be the fall guy? I'm off,' he said hurriedly. 'I'll see you in late August, sister dear. I'm not waiting around to be blamed for this little fiasco! And if you're wise, you won't either!'

'But, Daniel,' Bryony began, bewildered, as her brother gave her a swift hug and a kiss on the cheek. 'You can't just leave!'

'Oh, yes, I can.' With another hug, he turned on his heel and left.

'Daniel!' she exclaimed, hurrying after him. 'Where are you going?'

'Anywhere away from here.' With a remarkably cheerful wave, he pushed out through the swing doors and was immediately swallowed up by the crowds outside.

Slowly retracing her steps, a puzzled look on her lovely face, Bryony went to hover uncertainly beside Dries and his niece.

'Where's your brother gone?' he asked suspiciously.

'I don't know,' she confessed quietly.

'No,' he murmured, and the look he gave her said it all: Now judge for yourself. Is this a girl who's bad?

The trouble was, Bryony was no longer sure that Clare hadn't been the innocent party—and hated herself for doubting her brother—yet, despite the noisy sobs the girl had been indulging in, not one streak of mascara marred her smooth cheek, nor was there the faintest trace of a puffy eyelid, or a red nose, and Bryony frowned. Yet even if Daniel had been telling the truth, it wasn't a game either of them was going to win. She could see that very clearly.

'Hello Clare,' she greeted the girl despondently.

'Hello,' whispered Clare. She sounded sweet and injured. 'Are you Danny's sister?'

'Yes.'

'He doesn't like me,' Clare complained pathetically, her eyes wide and innocent. Too wide and innocent? Bryony wondered.

'No,' she agreed. Well, what else could she say? Daniel didn't like Clare. 'What made you take off from

Penang in such a hurry?' she asked curiously.

Looking down—her eyelashes not even damp, Bryony saw—Clare fiddled with the edge of her T-shirt. 'I panicked,' she whispered. 'When the clerk gave me Dries's note, I was terrified! I thought he'd be so angry . . .' Peeping up at her uncle, she gave him a tremulous smile. 'I thought I could get back to school before he caught up with me. I've been an awful nuisance, haven't I?' With an artistry that belonged before the cameras, the beautiful blue eyes filled with tears. They welled slowly up and overflowed one by one to trickle down the beautiful face.

Oh, how I wish I could do that, Bryony yearned, it's so effective. 'Why didn't you book a flight yesterday, when you arrived?' she asked.

'Bryony!' Dries exclaimed. 'Not now!'

Glancing at him, she gave in, and with a rather cynical smile that sat so oddly on her beautiful face she murmured, 'No, not now. I'll go and register. You and Clare will have a lot to talk about.'

'Yes,' he agreed. 'I'm sorry that Daniel——'

'Oh, don't be,' she sighed, knowing exactly what he was going to say, and knowing too that he wasn't sorry—why should he be? 'I know when I'm on a loser. The Grant family's weapons aren't nearly so effective.'

When he frowned, she gave him a lame smile. 'Don't worry about it, our backs are broad.'

'I do wish you wouldn't talk in riddles,' he complained irritably.

'Yes, I know, but in this instance I think it's probably best.'

'You don't want to hear Clare's explanation?'

'No, Dries. I really don't think I do. Sorry, Clare,'

Bryony said, turning to his niece, and just for a moment, she saw a look of triumph flitter across the young face. Just for an instant, and then it was gone. 'No,' she repeated slowly, 'I think I prefer to believe Daniel's version.'

'Even if it isn't the truth?'

Staring at him, wondering if she had imagined the note of disappointment in his voice, then deciding that she probably had, she shook her head. With an unhappy ache inside, and too tired to play verbal games, she turned away to the desk.

'But you don't know their explanations don't tally!' he exclaimed, the irritation noticeably pronounced.

'Oh, but I do—I could even give a very good guess at Clare's version. Daniel persuaded Clare, naturally against her better judgement, and when she arrived in Hong Kong, still reluctant and unsure, of course, she found he wasn't a bit as she remembered him; she was miserable and lonely, and if it hadn't been for the other students looking after her . . .' Turning to Clare, Bryony raised one eyebrow. 'How am I doing?'

More gentle tears, an unhappy nod of the head, and Bryony gave an appreciative little smile. Oh, Clare was good, very, very good, she should have been on the stage—and she loved the 'Lady Macbeth' type hand-wringing, that was a masterly stroke.Shaking her head, she went to register.

Tipping the bellboy, who insisted on carrying her meagre luggage up to her room, she dumped her rucksack on the bed before going across to the window to stare blindly down at the street below. Sorry, Daniel, she mentally apologised, for doubting you for even a moment, yet to plead your innocence now, I'd be batting off a very sticky wicket; then she turned and stared thoughtfully at the door as someone knocked. Dries, or Clare? Walking across, she slowly opened it. Clare.

'Yes?' she asked unhelpfully.

With a look of defiance that Bryony found a great deal more forgivable than the performance enacted downstairs, Clare said aggressively, 'Danny deserves everything I say about him—and, no matter whether you deny it or not, Dries won't believe you.'

'Oh, I know that,' Bryony said quietly. 'I'm not entirely stupid, but just out of interest why does Daniel deserve it?'

'Because in Paris, he let me think he liked me, a lot, that it would be fun if I came out. But when I arrived, he was furious. He treated me like a little kid! Well, I showed him!' said Clare vindictively, proving just what a child she still was, 'and if you get in my way or try to cause trouble, I'll show you! I can make up all sorts of stories about your precious brother!'

'I'm sure you can,' Bryony said mildly, 'Goodbye, Clare,' Without waiting for her to leave, she closed the door in the girl's face and leaned wearily against it. Poor Daniel, who'd only wanted to get on with his holiday in peace. Poor Clare, who'd expected the trip of a lifetime, excitement and romance,and had found only indifference. A spoilt little girl who expected everyone to love her. And poor Bryony, who was piggy in the middle. Oh, to hell with it, she thought tiredly. This little piggy's going out to explore Singapore. If she sat in her room she would only get more and more miserable; walking would at least give her some exercise and keep her out of Dries's way.

Feeling thoroughly fed up, she shoved some money into her pocket and went downstairs. Leaving her key at the desk, she went hastily out, hoping against hope she wouldn't encounter Dries or Clare.

Wandering aimlessly round the crowded streets, she stared blankly at ornate temples that seemed to huddle incongruously between skyscrapers, her mind on Clare. Poor little rich girl, and such a horrid age to be. Neither child nor adult. What were her parents like? she wondered. Indifferent? Strait-laced, Dries had said. Was that why they had bundled her off to finishing school? Because she'd become too much to handle? And had she fared any better with Daniel? Bryony wondered despondently. He'd been rude and aggressive to Dries, quite obviously scathing and impatient with Clare. I want to go home, she thought. Back to my quiet little life where nothing happens and the only decisions I have to make are what materials to use. Yet despite Daniel's behaviour, was it fair to allow him to be blamed? Yet if she defended him, they'd be another row, more constraint between Dries and herself.

Her eyes blank, her thoughts turned inward, Bryony stared at the sights and saw only bright blue eyes, could almost feel the thickness of his dark blond hair, feel the strength of his hard body—and she wanted him, dammit! Wanted to throw herself into his arms and let him love her. And she couldn't! Coming to an abrupt halt, she screwed her eyes tight shut until she'd got herself under control. Don't think about him. Think about Clare, about deceptively innocent blue eyes and golden curls.

The famous Raffles Hotel, that had been a must on her mental list of places to see, was just a building; the Botanical Gardens became a meaningless blur of colour. She should have made Clare explain in front

of Dries instead of putting words in her mouth. She
should have tried guile; she should have tried a few
tears of her own—in fact, what she should have done
was watch where she was walking, because then she
wouldn't have tried to squeeze into the gap between
two stalls that even an idiot would have known wasn't
wide enough.

Even then it might have been all right if she hadn't
been wearing her trousers with the wide pockets, but
she was, and was brought rather violently back to the
present as her pocket caught the bolt that held the
upright of the canopy in place and yanked it free. As
the whole structure gave an ominous wobble, she
frantically grabbed the frame with both hands. Oh,
hell, why did these things always happen to her?
Peering down between her outstretched arms in an
effort to locate the bolt, she gave a groan of despair as
she saw it lying under the stall just out of reach of her
foot. Wasn't that just typical? Sorely tempted to let go
and run, she shrieked in fright when someone tapped
her on the shoulder.

'For God's sake, Dries, you nearly gave me a heart
attack!' she exclaimed.

'It's nothing to what I'd like to give you,' he gritted
savagely. 'Where the hell have you been? I've been
turning this damned town upside-down looking for
you—and why the devil are you hiding in here?'

'I'm not hiding,' she said, exasperated, 'and will
you please keep your voice down!'

'Why?'

'Because I don't want everyone round here to see
what we're up to!'

'We're not up to anything!' he denied violently.

'Yes, we are! And I do wish you'd remember that

I'm twenty-seven and quite capable of taking care of myself! Dries!' she called frantically as he turned away. 'Come back here!'

'Why?' he asked nastily. 'You just told me you could take care of yourself.'

'Well, I can, usually,' Bryony mumbled awkwardly, 'only now that you're here I need your help.'

'Oh, do you? Well, isn't that a shame?'

'Oh, will you stop being difficult?' she snapped. 'I'm not leaning against this stall for the good of my health, you know!'

'Then why are you leaning against it?' he asked silkily, rocking backwards and forwards on his heels, a horrid expression of superiority on his face.

'Because I'm holding it up!' she gritted.

His rocking movement abruptly halted, Dries stared at her and slowly took his hands out of his pockets. 'What?' he demanded.

'I'm holding it up,' she mumbled. 'The bolt fell out.'

'Oh, God!'

'Yes—well, do you think that instead of invoking the help of the Deity, you could put it back? If I let go, the whole thing will fall over, and I don't think the stallholder would be very pleased.'

'I'm pretty sure he wouldn't, it's stacked high with crockery.'

'I know it is! Where are you going?' she yelped in horror as he turned away. 'Don't you dare be so mean!'

'Why? It's what you deserve.'

'What do you mean it's what I deserve? What the hell have I done?'

'What the hell haven't you done? And I'm very,

very tempted to leave you to stew in your own juice.'
Staring rather grimly at her, Dries suddenly gave a
long drawn-out sigh and let his shoulders slump.
'Even for you, Bryony, this has to be a classic. How
the hell did the bolt fall out?'

'Well, it wasn't witchcraft! I was just walking past,
minding my own business——'

'You never mind your own business,' he retorted
squashingly. 'Where's the bolt now?'

'Down there—it rolled under the stall. And please
hurry, this thing's heavy!' she said urgently.

'Serves you right,' he retorted, but to her relief he
bent to retrieve the bolt and, moving her out the way
with his hip, slotted it back in. 'All right, you can let
go now.'

Gingerly taking her hands away, Bryony held her
breath as the stall swayed, then steadied. 'Thank you,'
she said grudgingly.

'Oh, you're so welcome,' Dries retorted
sarcastically. 'And now perhaps you'd tell me why
you were so rude to Clare.'

'Me rude?' she squeaked in disbelief. '*Me*?'

'Yes, you. I couldn't believe it when she told me.'

'Told you what?' she demanded aggressively.

'That she'd come to your room to apologise and you
bit her head off.'

'Oh, is that why she came? How odd, I thought she
came to warn me off.'

'Warn you off what?' he asked, looking thoroughly
confused.

'Oh, don't be stupid!' Bryony retorted, stamping her
foot in frustration. 'And what was she supposed to be
apologising for? I thought she was the innocent party!'

'She was!'

'Ooh . . .' Tempted to say a very rude word, she contented herself with a sniff of disgust and stalked past him. Thankfully she saw their hotel just up the road and, her mouth tight, she ran lightly up the steps and pushed inside. Clare was hovering in the foyer, and for once, Bryony's temper overcame her usual desire for peace at any price. Marching up to her, she said rudely, 'You should write a book, sweetheart, fiction seems to be your forte.'

Pushing her out of the way, she went to get her key, then halted when Clare put a tentative hand on her arm. 'Yes?' she asked aggressively, then gave a nasty smile when she saw the reason for this little display of contrition. Dries was standing about two feet away.

'I am sorry,' Clare said sweetly.

'Oh, are you? Forgive me if I find that a little hard to swallow—and if you're about to embark on another piece of fiction, don't bother, I've heard quite enough stories for one day!'

Brushing rudely past her, intent only on escape before she did something totally stupid like strangle the girl, Bryony was halted again by Dries's exasperated voice.

'What the hell is the matter with you?' he demanded.

'Nothing is the matter with me!' she snapped.

'No, it doesn't sound like it! And might I remind you that I at least had the courtesy to listen to your brother's explanation. Can't you be generous enough to show Clare the same consideration?'

'Courtesy?' she yelled, quite uncaring that they had now become the focus of all eyes in the foyer. 'You condemned him out of hand! You'd made up your mind about his guilt before you even met him! Oh, for

God's sake!' she exploded as she realised that her
words weren't even registering. Glaring at him,
wishing she had something to wallop him with, like a
tank, she made a frustrated noise in the back of her
throat and headed for the stairs. She should have gone
with Daniel, she thought furiously. She should have
gone home. Slamming into her room, she kicked
moodily at the rug as she walked across to the armchair
and threw herself into it. Why were men so
monumentally stupid? Couldn't they see what was
under their noses? No, of course they couldn't. With
an irritable little gesture, she picked her sketchpad up
off the bed and flipped over the pages. Grabbing her
pencil from the bedside cabinet she began a wicked
caricature of viper Clare, then set her mouth
mutinously when the door opened behind her.

'Right,' Dries said briskly, 'I'd like an explanation.
Clare has gone out of her way to be polite to you——'

'Oh, don't be so dumb!' Bryony snapped.

'And don't you be so damned rude! What the hell
is the matter with you?'

'Nothing.'

'Then stop sulking!'

'I am not sulking!' she yelled.

'Yes, you are! I brought you on this trip for the
express purpose of helping me with Clare—and what
do you do? Make everything ten times more difficult!
I don't know anything about teenagers,' Dries
complained aggrievedly as he walked across to lean
on the back of her chair and peer over her shoulder,
'and the least you could do is help me with her!'

Petulantly snapping her pad shut, she gritted, 'The
only thing I'd help you to do with her is strangle her!
So go away, I don't want to talk to you.'

'Tough. I'm staying right here until you tell me why the hell you're behaving like a spoilt child.'

'Oh, the saints preserve me!' With an abrupt movement that took him by surprise, Bryony got to her feet, and with her weight removed the chair tipped over backwards, sending Dries sprawling.

'Serves you right,' she said unfeelingly, then squealed in alarm as he grabbed her ankle and pulled her down on top of him. 'Let me go!'

'No. Not until you apologise.'

'Apologise?' she exclaimed. 'For what? I didn't tell you to lean on the back of my chair!'

'I wasn't talking about the chair.'

'Well, I'm not going to apologise for being rude to Clare! She deserved it—and if you can't see when you're being taken for a ride, then I'm sure as hell not going to point it out to you! And if I were you,' she added furiously, 'I'd leave before the little dear catches you in my room!'

'And why should I mind if she catches me?'

'Because . . .oh, because, ' she said crossly, unable to think of an acceptable explanation.

'Very articulate,' he taunted, his blue eyes hard as he continued to hold her captive.

'I hate you!' she spat, wriggling agitatedly in an effort to escape.

'No, you don't—and keep still.'

'No! Let me go!'

'No.' Clamping one hand round the back of her neck, Dries glared at her, then, with a sound that closely approximated a groan, he forced her mouth to his, and because she wasn't expecting it she wasn't fast enough rallying her defences. Making mutinous little noises in the back of her throat, she tried to force herself away from him, terrified that if she didn't break away soon she was going to respond, because, whatever she might think of him personally, her wretched body didn't seem to agree. Already she was melting, her thoughts blurring, and she made one last almighty effort to get away.

'Damn you, Bryony, keep still!' grated Dries, and with a heave of his body he turned them both over so that she was beneath him.

'No, I won't keep still! I don't want you to kiss me!'

'Yes, you do.'

'No, I don't! Don't be so damned arrogant—and might I remind you that it was you who started all this nonsense, not me?'

'Do you think that makes it any easier?' he demanded. Ignoring her defiance, he bent his head and kissed her again and again until her traitorous body was weak and melting; until she couldn't think straight; until she wanted to kiss him back, until the effort of denying herself became a physical pain. 'Kiss me,' he persuaded gruffly. 'Let me make love to you. You never know, you might enjoy it.'

'I won't,' Bryony said obdurately, her eyes stormy, her voice breathless and uneven. 'You've been nothing but trouble since the day I met you and——'

'And you don't want to be troubled, do you?'

'No.'

'Such a coward!' he taunted.

'That's not the point!'

'Oh, but it is.' Sliding one large palm round to her jaw, he traced her lower lip with his thumb. He looked confused and reluctant, she thought, which hardly helped to ease her own confusion, and when he lowered his head and brought his mouth to within a hair's breadth of hers she hastily closed her eyes. 'It's very much the point,' he growled, and the movement of his lips on hers as he spoke sent a little quiver of excitement through her. 'Although, believe it or not,' he continued with a funny little sigh, 'I only came to talk to you.' Drawing back, he looked down into her lovely, flushed face. 'It's becoming an awful obsession, this wanting to make love to you.' Rolling away from her, he hunched up into a sitting position, arms between his knees, hands linked round his ankles. 'Looks like another cold shower,' he muttered with a lame attempt at humour.

Uncertain and aching, Bryony almost gave in; it was a terrible temptation to say yes. Putting out a tentative hand to touch his back, she drew away startled when he flinched. 'Don't push your luck, sweetheart,' he pleaded on a breath dragged deep into his lungs, 'this is a borderline case,' Turning his head, he surveyed her worried face and a small reluctant smile danced in his eyes. 'I'm not used to practising self-restraint— although to be honest I've never wanted anyone as I want you, so it was never a problem—and there's absolutely no need to point out that it's my own fault!'

'I wasn't going to,' she denied quietly. Moving to a sitting position and clasping her arms round her updrawn knees, she sighed miserably. 'Oh, Dries, what is it about you? There seems to be a very real danger of my falling in love with you—and I don't want that! Neither do you, do you?'

'No,' he said quietly.

'I know it's only a fun thing for you, a diversion, but I can't be like that, Dries! I tried, and I can't! Other women do, have, I mean——'

'Oh, shut up,' he said without heat, 'and it sure as

hell doesn't feel like a fun thing at the moment. The hell of it is, that's probably why I like you so much.'

'Because it isn't fun?' she asked, confused.

'No,' he denied on a grunt of laughter, 'because you're such an innocent.'

'Or because it's a want-what-you-can't-have syndrome?' Bryony asked softly.

'No, the wanting of a very beautiful, funny lady whose every movement is an unconscious come-on.' Pressing both hands down on his knees, Dries levered himself to his feet. 'Doe's eyes,' he murmured, staring down at her, 'You didn't have any lunch.'

'No, I wasn't very hungry.'

'Then we'll have an early dinner.'

'No,' she denied hastily, 'I'll have something sent up to my room, have an early night.' She really couldn't face the thought of sitting opposite a smug Clare.

'All right, I'll say goodnight, then.' With an odd little smile, he added, 'And I have the very uncharitable thought that I hope you sleep as badly as I know I will.'

She probably would, Bryony thought, sighing despondently as the door closed behind him. Regret already filled her, and not making love to him wasn't going to make it any easier when they went their separate ways, so she might just as well have given in, mightn't she? And what did he mean about her unintentional behaviour? Come-on, indeed! What a revolting expression, and it wasn't in the least true, she thought moodily.

Getting to her feet, she walked across to stare from the window. She didn't even understand why Dries was being so persistent. He didn't seem at all the sort of man to pursue a lost cause—especially as that cause was related to the boy he thought had tried to get his niece into bed with him, or at least she supposed that was what he thought. She hadn't really any idea what Clare had told him. And, come to think of it, his behaviour was very little different from what he presumably supposed Daniel's to be. Perhaps that was why he hadn't had a go at her about it.

Sighing, even more confused, Bryony thumped her fist down on the window-sill. She didn't want to feel like this! Surely all it should have taken was mind over matter? If you don't want, ergo, you won't. All you have to do, Bryony Grant, is stay resolute, she told herself firmly, and have a cold shower—which was all very well if only the effect didn't wear off as soon as you were warm again. Perhaps she'd go and have a drink in the bar; that would make her feel better, wouldn't it? On an empty stomach? she taunted herself. Why not? Getting drunk might at least ensure that she slept. Walking rather disconsolately down to the bar, she ordered a gin and tonic, then sat in solitary splendour watching the ice cubes revolve. Oh, what a lovely way to spend an evening, she sang softly to herself, then gave a gurgle of laughter. Bryony Grant, you're a fool! Oh, yes. Draining the contents of her glass quickly, she returned the empty glass to the bar, intending to go back to her room. As she crossed the lobby, a movement seen from the corner of her eye made her turn her head curiously, and she was just in time to see Clare sneaking out, dressed up to the nines.

Oh, God, where was she off to in such a hurry? Torn between her desire to protect Dries and her desire to see Clare get her come-uppance, Bryony hurried after her, plumping for Dries's peace of mind. Although goodness knew why she should, after the things he'd said to her. But Clare was only a child, when all was said and done, and Bryony's conscience wouldn't allow her to let the girl go blithely off into the night in a strange town. Anything might happen to her.

She had just pushed through the swing doors when a heavy hand fell on her shoulder.

'Oh, no, my girl, you are not, positively not, going sightseeing at this hour,' Dries drawled softly from behind her.

'I wasn't going sightseeing,' she denied fatalistically, and what demon had prompted him to arrive at just this particular moment in time? 'You have lousy timing, Dries du Vaal,' she told him irritably. 'However, all is perhaps not lost. If we hurry we can catch her up . . .'

'Catch who up?'

'Clare, of course. I just saw her sneaking . . . Yes!' she said in exasperation when he shook his head.

'No, I spoke to Clare not five minutes ago in her room. She's going to have an early night. Oh, Bryony, are you really that blinkered where Daniel's concerned?' he asked sadly.

'Daniel?' she asked, confused. 'What's Daniel got to do with it?'

'This vendetta against Clare! This trying to prove that she isn't innocent! Can't you be honest enough to admit that he's, if not wholly, then at least partially to blame? I know how fond of him you are, but covering up for him won't do any good in the long run. Maybe you were too lenient with him or he had too much money too soon—but, whatever the reason, surely Clare doesn't deserve this vindictiveness?'

'This what?' Bryony asked in disbelief. Staring at

him, at the utter conviction on his face that he was right, she closed her eyes for a moment, unbearably hurt that he could think such a thing of her. 'Dries,' she murmured lifelessly, 'I'm not waging a vendetta, neither did Daniel lie. Your niece did. Believe me, those baby blue eyes of hers hide a brain every bit as inventive as Machiavelli's. She is not tucked up safely in her bed. She is sneaking off round the back streets of Singapore—and I am going to find her before she lands us in any more trouble!'

'No, you aren't. You, Bryony Grant, are going up to your room!'

'No, I'm not!' she denied, exasperated.

'Bryony,' he said with dangerous softness, 'you are not going out.' And to reinforce his words, he caught hold of her arm in a very firm grip. 'No arguments, no discussions, you're going up to your room, or the bar, or the dining-room, or anywhere in the hotel, but you're not going out.'

'Dries,' she said wearily, 'once before you didn't believe me . . .'

His eyes examining hers, he gave a long sigh of defeat. 'Oh, God. Which way did she go?'

'That way,' she said, indicating to the right.

Altering his grip on her arm, he hurried with her along the narrow pavement. 'If you're lying to me, Bryony . . .' he grated.

'Why in heaven's name would I be lying?' she asked, incensed.

'Lord knows. But if she's sneaked out to meet your brother——'

'Oh, for God's sake!' she exploded, wrenching her arm from his. 'You go and find her, then! She's your niece!'

'All right, all right,' he surrendered, 'I'm sorry. We'll both go and find her.'

It took them two hours, by which time Dries's patience and most of his cash had long since run out. 'I'll tell you something,' he said wrathfully as they pushed through the beaded curtain into a nightclub inappropriately called the Convent Garden and thrust some money into the doorman's hand, 'I am never, ever, going to have children! What with you and Clare, I'm beginning to feel like a bloody sheep-dog!'

'Well, how the hell do you think I feel?' Bryony exploded. She was hot and hungry and tired and her feet hurt. And her head. How the hell could people come to places like this night after night to be bombarded by coloured lights and music that was loud enough to deafen one? Five minutes in one of these clubs was enough to convince her that she would never, ever become a social animal, if these were the sort of places she'd be expected to frequent.

Stepping down on to the edge of the dance-floor, she was brought up short by a firm grasp on the back of her shirt.

'What?' she asked impatiently.

'Over there,' Dries said quietly.

Staring in the direction he indicated, Bryony felt her heart sink. Clare was standing in the corner, her back to them, talking to Daniel. Wishing a benign God would swoop down and spirit her away, she trailed miserably after Dries's tall figure. What the hell was Daniel doing here?

'Outside!' Dries said peremptorily to them both. 'Now!'

Clare looked frightened and meekly went with her

uncle. Daniel looked as though he were about to argue, but Bryony grabbed his arm, her eyes pleading. With a shrug, he followed the others outside.

'Right! What were you doing there?' Dries demanded, staring grimly at Daniel, his hands shoved into his jeans pockets as though needing to physically restrain himself from hitting him.

'I saw Madam Clare go in and followed to see what she was up to——'

'You liar!' screamed Clare. 'You invited me! Asked me to meet you here before I got sent back tomorrow!'

'Shut up!' thundered Dries, and when Clare subsided he asked softly, 'Is this true?'

'No,' Daniel said, lounging back against the wall, a look of boredom on his thin face.

'It is, it is,' Clare whispered, clinging on to Dries's arm. 'He said it would only take five minutes,' she gabbled. 'He wanted to talk to me, he said, and I waited and waited outside, and it was horrible,' she gasped, throwing herself into Dries's arms. 'Men kept trying to pick me up . . .'

Thrusting her not ungently away from him, he advanced on Daniel, his face grimmer than Bryony had ever seen it.

'No!' she yelled, pushing Clare aside. 'Don't you dare touch him!'

'Shut up!' he grated savagely.

'No, I won't shut up!' Forcing herself between them, Bryony stood with her back to her brother, her arms spread protectively wide. Both men were a good head taller than she was. She looked ridiculous, and she didn't care. 'You lay one finger on him and I'll—I'll . . .'

'You'll what?' Dries asked derisively. Picking her

up, he moved her to one side. 'Take Clare back to the hotel.'

'I will not!'

'You'll do as you're damned well told!' he thundered, his temper finally breaking his self-imposed bounds. 'And, for someone who can't cope with rows and arguments, you're suddenly doing a pretty fine job, aren't you? Or was that just a ploy? Was it, Bryony?' he demanded furiously.

'No, it was not!' she said forcefully, 'but I didn't say I didn't have a temper! And when I lose it, I get very, very brave! Now let go of my damned arm!'

'No!' As he stared at her, his expression suddenly changed to one of deep consideration, and she felt a little *frisson* of alarm. She didn't think she quite liked the way he was looking at her.

'Let me go,' she whispered, her eyes fixed widely on his face.

'No. How wrong have I been about you Bryony Grant? Because I did wonder, you know, how you'd managed to reach the age of twenty-seven and remain such an innocent—hah!' he exclaimed when she flushed. 'So where else have I been led down the garden path? Your insistence on coming to look for Clare alone? You knew she was meeting Daniel, didn't you?'

'No!'

Ignoring her denial, he continued softly, 'You'd go to any lengths to protect your brother, wouldn't you?'

'She doesn't need to go to any lengths,' Daniel said coldly, levering himself away from the wall and doing a bit of grabbing of his own, 'and let go of her arm. And, instead of blaming everyone but yourself, you'd do better to ask your precious niece why the hell I would want to meet her when I don't even like her!'

'Because I only have your word for it that you don't!' Dries gritted. 'And, now I come to think of it, it seems very suspicious that the minute I decided to come to Bangkok, you decided to high-tail it somewhere else!' Swinging back on Bryony, he said nastily, 'You warned him, didn't you?'

'No, I did not! How could I have warned him?'

'How the hell should I know? Oh, I can understand it, I suppose,' he continued wearily. 'You practically brought him up, you felt the need to protect him——'

'No! That isn't true. And I certainly wouldn't have protected him if he'd been in the wrong! He helped us search for her, damn it! Why would he do that if he was as you say he is?'

'Guilt,' Dries said succinctly, 'only his sister doesn't seem to feel the same emotions, does she? It becomes very clear now why you flirted with me——'

'Me flirt?' she exclaimed in disbelief. '*Me*?'

'Yes, you. To take my mind off your brother!'

'Well, if that doesn't beat all! Who was it dragged me into a flower-scented bower? The Invisible Man? And why? If you believed Daniel was a seducer of young girls, why try to seduce his sister?'

'I was not trying to seduce you!' he yelled. 'I liked you! Believed you were acting out of innocence! Only you weren't, were you? So what else have you lied about, I wonder?'

'I haven't lied about anything! And quite frankly I don't give a damn whether you believe me or not!' Wrenching her arm free, Bryony whirled away from him and began walking back to the hotel, her breath coming in sobbing gasps.

'And what,' Daniel asked quietly from beside her,

'was that all about?'

'Nothing! And I hope your niece gets had up for soliciting!' she turned to shout childishly over her shoulder at Dries, who was following close at their heels, Clare held firmly by one arm.

'Yes! That's the real Bryony talking, isn't it?' he gritted, grabbing her again. 'You'd rather see a young girl get herself into trouble than admit your precious brother is at fault! Well, maybe he learned by association, maybe it's unfair to blame him—you brought him up, after all.'

'You bastard! That's a lousy thing to say!'

'Is it?' he asked coldly. 'Or is it too close to the truth?'

Staring at him, her small face pinched and white, her stomach churning, Bryony whispered brokenly, 'Don't you ever, ever come near me again. Don't you touch me or speak to me or anything!'

Dragging herself free, grabbing Daniel, she marched them both along the road. She was breathing so hard it made her ribs ache. 'And you were a fat lot of help,' she denigrated tearfully to her brother. 'Thanks a lot!'

'You didn't need my help,' he murmured, suddenly sounding amused, 'you seemed to be doing very well on your own.'

'Don't you even care what he thinks of you?' she exploded in disbelief.

'No, why should I? I haven't done anything. And if you were expecting a champion, don't please look at me.'

'You rotten coward!' she snapped.

'Bryony! He's twice my size!'

'So? You could have tried!'

'And get myself pulverised? No, thank you. And now, my sweet sister,' Daniel added, halting and indicating that they had reached her hotel, 'I will wish you adieu.' Searching her wan face with rather more intensity than she could have wished for, he exclaimed suddenly, 'Oh, my God—you're in love with him!' A broad grin spreading across his face, he began to laugh.

'I am not!' she yelled, walloping him as hard as she could across the arm. 'I hate him! Goodbye!' Rushing up the hotel steps, her face white with shock, Daniel's words ringing in her ears, she dashed up to her room and slammed the door. She was shaking so badly she could barely stand. Lowering herself to the floor, her back against the door, she stared down at her updrawn feet through a blur of tears. She didn't love Dries, she didn't! And why was it, she asked herself wrathfully, that she always did the very thing she'd told herself not to do? Don't get involved with him, she'd told herself, you won't be able to cope. And she couldn't. Despite Dries's obvious disbelief that rows upset her, it was true. Even if she managed to defend herself at the time, afterwards she always went to pieces.

Suddenly hearing footsteps outside in the corridor, and a furiously whispered conversation, she froze, then shot to her feet and retreated across the room, her wide fearful eyes fixed on the door.

'Go away!' she called hoarsely as the door crashed open to reveal Dries. He had the look of a man who had finally come to the conclusion that hanging was a price he would willingly pay. 'I feel sick!'

As he advanced into the room, dragging a terrified looking Clare with him, Bryony backed up to the window and stood pressed up against it like a cornered animal.

'You feel sick!' he derided harshly. 'How the hell do you think I feel? Apart from the little matter of providing a free side-show for half the population of Singapore, I now discover your bloody brother has been introducing my niece to drugs! That will really go down well with her father, won't it?'

'No!' screamed Clare, rushing across to grab his arm. 'You're not to tell Daddy! You promised!'

'I did not promise!' he gritted, shrugging her off. 'You think I can keep quiet about something like that? You think I can leave your wretched Daniel Grant to peddle death around the Far East?'

'Drugs?' Bryony whispered, her face losing what little colour it had left. 'Daniel doesn't use drugs.'

'I didn't say he used them.'

Staring at him, feeling sick and ill, she pressed shaking hands to her chest where her heart seemed to be fluttering unevenly. 'Oh, you fool,' she breathed, her voice barely audible. Turning only her head, she stared at Clare. 'Do you really hate him so much that you'd see him rot in some gaol? All because your little adventure turned sour? Would you?'

Looking every bit as sick and frightened as Bryony, Clare turned and made a bolt for the door—and ran slap into Daniel. He grabbed her arms, turned her around and shoved her across the bed.

He looks like a stranger, Bryony thought numbly. Grown up. His thin face was taut and angry as he slammed the door behind him. 'I decided,' he began quietly, 'that it wasn't fair to let Bryony take the blame. So I came back. I followed them up the stairs.' Turning to look at the weeping Clare sprawled across the bed, he said coldly, 'Drugs?'

'No,' she sobbed, her voice muffled in the bedspread.

Walking across to her, he yanked her over on to her back. 'Drugs?' he repeated. 'I've taken a lot from you the last few weeks, Clare. Your tantrums, your screaming fits, your sulking—and, all right, maybe I didn't handle it as well as I might have done. Maybe I did inadvertently allow you to believe I wouldn't mind if you came out here, and I probably wouldn't if you hadn't turned out to be such a bitch. But drugs, Clare?'

'I said no!' she shrieked, sounding almost hysterical.

'That isn't what you said on the stairs to your precious uncle. Now tell him the truth—all of it!'

'There weren't any drugs,' she mumbled.

'And the rest of it,' Daniel commanded, dragging her into a sitting position when she remained silent. 'Go on!'

'I went out to meet Martin and John, two of the students.'

'But not me,' Daniel persisted.

'No.'

Giving her a last look of disgust, he straightened and looked at Dries. 'Satisfied?'

His eyes distant, bleak, Dries looked down at his niece.

'Well?' Daniel demanded.

With a long, deep sigh, Dries turned to look at him. 'Yes,' he said quietly, 'I'm satisfied. Get up, Clare,' he added coldly, returning his attention to the sobbing girl. When she didn't move, he grabbed her arm and yanked her upright. 'Now apologise.'

With a little whimper, her head hung, she

whispered, 'Sorry.'

'Sorry?' Dries echoed. Looking up at Daniel, his blue eyes holding the younger man's, he gave a grim smile. 'I seem to have been doing rather a lot of misjudging lately, don't I? I'm sorry, Daniel.' His face grey in the artificial light, he turned to look at Bryony.

Jerking her eyes away, she stared down at her clasped hands and prayed for him to go. As soon as she heard the door click to, she closed her eyes and collapsed back against the wall.

'Are you all right?' Daniel asked gently, walking across to her and stooping to look into her white face.

Nodding, a mere jerk of her head, she gave a little sniff and tried to smile at him. Only her mouth wouldn't obey her command, so she nodded again, little shivers racking her.

'Need me to stay?'

Shaking her head, she stared back at her clasped hands.

'Poor devil,' Daniel muttered, 'I feel quite sorry for him. What will you do?'

'Go home,' she whispered.

'Want me to come with you?'

'No,' she denied, giving him a wobbly smile. 'But thank you for asking. I'm sorry I didn't allow you to grow up . . .'

'You did, Brains—oh, now don't cry.' Taking her awkwardly in his arms, Daniel added, 'I'd better stay.'

'No,' she said, wriggling out of his hold. 'Go and enjoy your holiday.' Making one last effort, she turned him round and propelled him towards the door. 'Go!'

'Sure?'

'Sure. I'm all right now. I'm going to bed, and in the morning I'll fly home. Give me a ring next week.'

'Well, all right, if you're sure——'

'I am. Go!'

With a relieved smile, he went.

Walking across to the bed, Bryony curled up on the cover, the pillow hugged to her stomach. She felt awful, light-headed and ill, and she was shaking so badly she felt sick.

It was maybe an hour later when she heard the soft tap on her door. Dries, she supposed, with an explanation, an apology. Ignoring it, she curled tighter against the pillow and closed her eyes, pretending sleep. She heard the door open, soft footsteps moving towards the bed, and forced herself to breathe deeply, evenly. After what seemed an eternity, the footsteps retreated and the door was closed quietly. Burying her face in the pillow, she began to cry quietly, and eventually drifted into sleep.

When she went down to breakfast the next morning, her face still white, dark shadows beneath her lovely eyes, she came face to face with Dries at the bottom of the stairs. He had obviously been waiting for her.

'Bryony——' he began.

'I don't want to talk about it,' she interrupted quickly, staring rigidly at his chest. 'I just want to go home.'

'I know. I've booked us on the noon flight.' Catching her arm, and moving her to stand to one side, he continued earnestly, 'I had a long talk with Clare last night—she isn't very popular at school, and I suppose in an attempt to make herself more interesting she boasted about her meeting with Daniel in Paris, about how he'd invited her to go to the Far East. No one believed her—so she had to go, just to prove them wrong. It doesn't excuse what she did——'

'No, it doesn't,' she burst out, her voice jerky and uneven, 'and I told you I don't want to talk about it. I'll go and pack.' Swinging away from him, she ran back upstairs. If she could just avoid him until they got back to England, she would be all right. She didn't want his explanations, want him to be humble, kind to her; she wanted him to ignore her, leave her alone.

Yet when he did as she wanted, and left her in peace, instead of feeling better, she felt worse, forlorn and lonely.

Squashed between Dries and Clare in the back of the taxi, Bryony kept her eyes fixed firmly on her lap. Dries had obviously given up trying to make her understand; Clare presumably didn't want her to, and she prayed she could find a seat on the flight away from them both.

With Murphy's Law being what it was, the flight was delayed, and they stood around the flight monitor like waxwork dummies, avoiding each other's glances. As soon as a bench became available Bryony went and sat down. The other two followed suit and they all sat like waxwork dummies. When the atmosphere became too fraught to withstand, Dries leapt to his feet with a muttered imprecation and went off to find out about the flight. Clare, obviously feeling she couldn't bear to be in such close proximity with someone who knew all her failings, got up and wandered away.

'Another half-hour,' muttered Dries, returning to stand in front of Bryony, hands jammed into his jeans pockets, and only then did he seem to notice that Clare wasn't there. 'Where the hell has she disappeared to?'

he demanded irritably, staring round him as though at any moment he expected some other drama to unfold.

'I don't know,' Bryony mumbled, then glared at him, daring him to blame her. With a scowl he swung away, then vented his bad temper on Clare, who chose that inauspicious moment to come back. 'Where the hell have you been?'

'Looking for something to do,' she whispered, her eyes filling with tears.

'Well, don't! And if you're thinking of wandering off, think again!' he said shortly, obviously not about to do or say anything that might be interpreted as softness. 'If you don't want to sit here, go and sit on that bench over there and wait.'

'I've said I was sorry,' she began tearfully. 'You don't need to treat me as though I'd just killed your dog!'

'Yes, I do,' he retorted, 'Now do as you're damned well told. God,' he muttered tiredly when Clare was out of earshot, 'if anything would deter me from having children, she would. How can someone who looks like that be a pathological liar?'

'She's only a child,' Bryony whispered, perversely wanting to defend the girl now that Dries was blaming her.

'Oh, don't you start!' he said disagreeably, then heaving an enormous sigh he ran a tired hand through his hair, 'I'm sorry. Look, we obviously can't talk here, but when we get back to . . . Now what?' he gritted as Clare came back to stand beside him.

'I need to go to the loo . . .'

'Oh, go!' he yelled, his temper finally exploding. 'And when you come back, don't bloody move until the flight is called!'

Oh, what a fun day, Bryony thought, beginning to

feel sick again. Just one jolly thing after another.

She managed to avoid them on the flight by taking a seat next to a dear little old lady who spent practically the whole fourteen hours regaling her with tales of her family, not one word of which Bryony remembered afterwards.

CHAPTER SIX

'I CAN get a cab, Dries,' Bryony said mutinously, and for at least the fourth time as they walked across the concourse at Heathrow. 'There is absolutely no need for you to go out of your way!'

'I said I'd take you and I will!'

'Oh, for God's sake, will you two stop arguing?' snapped Clare, obviously back on form. 'Let her get a damned cab! I don't care!'

'Well, I do! And if you don't shut up I'll put you over my knee! Now move, Bryony!'

'No!' Furious with herself and with Dries, Bryony picked up her rucksack and walked off towards the taxi-rank outside. She felt as though she were coming apart at the seams.

Her grand gesture cost her thirty pounds, but it was worth every penny not to have to be stuck in the car with the others. She needed peace and quiet and space to get herself back together again. Paying off the cab, she walked disconsolately up the path to her house. Five bottles of milk sat on the doorstep, and no doubt five newspapers would be lying inside on the mat. They were. She was surprised there were only five, it felt as though she'd been away for years. Tossing her rucksack down, she leaned tiredly back against the door, her eyes bleak. So that's that, she thought, *Finis*. Presumably what one might call half a light flirtation. Pushing away from the door, she went into the kitchen. No doubt the bread would be mouldy, the fridge full of out-of-date yoghurt and the butter rancid.

She'd also left the window open, she saw. How nice to be home!

Catching a glimpse of the clock, she saw with surprise that it was only eleven. A fourteen-hour flight, and it was only seven hours later than when they had finally left Singapore. She felt tired to death, but there didn't seem much point in going to bed. She knew she wouldn't be able to sleep, so she'd be better doing something constructive like clearing up the kitchen, however unattractive the prospect seemed. Yet when she had finished it was still only half past one and, although her body was exhausted, her mind wouldn't switch off. In fact, it kept coming up with the damnedest pieces of irrelevant information, like the fact that most suicides and deaths occurred between two and five in the morning. Hardly comforting.

Throwing herself moodily on to the sofa, Bryony stared blankly in front of her. What was Dries doing now? Sleeping? Had he shrugged her off like an old shoe? Why should it even matter? Yet it did, that was what she found so incomprehensible. She'd barely known him a week, yet he took up her thoughts to the exclusion of all else, leaving her miserable and confused and hurting. Partly her own fault, she knew. If she'd allowed him to apologise . . .but better to be miserable now than distraught later. Confucius, he say . . . Oh, shut up! She was still sitting there at five-thirty when someone hammered impatiently on the front door. With a sigh, she went to answer it; probably the milkman demanding to know whether she was setting up in competition.

Dragging open the front door, Bryony stared helplessly at Dries. 'What are you doing here?' she asked wearily. She didn't even seem to have the energy to feel angry. 'It would be a great deal better for everybody if you just left me alone.'

'No, it wouldn't,' he muttered, sounding every bit as fed up as she felt. Taking the door from her, he pushed into the hall, then nearly fell over the newspapers that she still hadn't picked up. Kicking them irritably to one side, he added disagreeably, 'There are five bottles of milk on your doorstep.'

'I know, I like them there. I thought I might start a collection.' Turning away from him before she did something totally stupid, like feel sorry for him, Bryony went back into the lounge, then, feeling twitchy and irritable and in no mood for a discussion on the whys and wherefores, she pushed through into her workshop and began fiddling absently with a piece of wood lying on the bench. 'I don't want you here,' she complained moodily, 'I'm tired.'

'So am I. Do you think you have a monopoly on it? I personally feel as though I haven't slept for a week.'

'Then you should have gone to bed,' she said unfeelingly. 'And what have you done with the dreaded Clare? You haven't brought her with you, have you?'

'No, I haven't! She's at my flat in London, and first thing tomorrow she'll be on a plane for Switzerland.'

'If she hasn't disappeared again while you're down here.'

'Well, if she has, she can stay disappeared!' he said crossly. 'And stop fiddling with that piece of wood! Anyway, I didn't come to talk about Clare. I came to apologise, explain.'

'I don't want you to apologise,' Bryony denied petulantly, tossing the piece of wood away when it broke in half. 'I've got a headache, and I don't want you to explain either—I don't think I care.'

'Well, I do,' Dries said grimly, 'so you'll bloody

well listen!'

'Huh!'

'Oh, shut up,' he said tiredly. Leaning back against the wall, he stared morosely at her before complaining, 'I don't even want to like you, and now look at me! I never explain things to people, they have to take me as they find me, and here I am behaving like . . . Oh, to hell with it. I'm sorry,' he admitted grudgingly.

'And that's it, is it?' she asked nastily.

'No, it isn't!' Marching across to her, he swung her round to face him, 'I'm sorry I accused your brother of all the things I accused him of, but hell, Bryony, how was I to know what Clare was like? I mean, damn it all! She looks as though——'

'Butter wouldn't melt in her mouth—yes, I know.But that's not the point.'

'I know it isn't the point!' he snapped, incensed. 'Will you please shut up and let me finish? And stop looking like a sulky child, it doesn't suit you.'

'How would you know? You've only known me a week, and take your hands off me, I'm not about to make a bolt for it.' Bryony said, twisting irritably away, although she sure as hell would have liked to. 'Oh, go on with it,' she instructed wearily as he resumed his position against the wall with a bad-tempered little twitch.

'I don't know where I got to——'

'Dries!'

'Well,' he muttered, sounding like the sulky child he'd accused her of being. 'And it wasn't entirely my fault, you know! Your blasted brother hardly helped!'

'Oh, that's it—accuse Daniel to hide your shortcomings!'

'I'm not accusing Daniel! I was only saying he

didn't help.'

'Well, whose fault was that? I told you and told you not to accuse him——'

'You did not!' he denied forcefully. 'And even if you had, did he need to be so obstructive?'

'What did you expect?' she parried, in no mood to admit that her brother was less than perfect. 'Going on and on at him—and I wasn't obstructive, but did that stop you having a go at me? No, it did not! And that's another thing,' she complained, incensed as she remembered just how awful that scene outside the nightclub had been. 'If Daniel was the one you thought to be at fault, why have a go at me? I was the innocent party in all this! I was just dragged along willy-nilly——'

'Oh, for God's sake!' Dries exploded, 'will you shut up? I was angry, hurt . . . I liked you, dammit! I didn't want you to be all those things I accused you of! I wanted to hurt you, make you pay! Clare said——'

'I know what Clare said! God, men can be so stupid somet——'

'I'll strangle you in a minute,' Dries said through his teeth, and Bryony subsided with a mutinous little sniff. 'I thought you'd lied to me,' he continued more calmly, 'and it hurt, Bryony, that you'd been stringing me along. And then on the way back to the hotel Clare told me she'd gone to meet Daniel because she was frightened of him, that he'd said if she didn't meet him he'd tell her father she was involved in the drug scene —I didn't stop to analyse it, I just reacted. I've seen first hand what drugs can do to people! The film industry seems riddled with them—youngsters who can't cope, who need a boost, whose careers have suddenly disintegrated. She's seventeen,' he burst out, 'and all I could see was the mess it would all become—our names dragged through the mud——'

'Oh, so that's it, is it?' Bryony asked sarcastically, determinedly squashing the sympathy that welled up in her. 'Never mind poor little Clare's life messed up with drugs! Never mind Daniel in gaol for peddling! All we have to worry about is our precious name dragged through the mud! And do you think the papers would care about some obscure Dutch family——?'

'We're not obscure, damn you!'

'Ah,' she exclaimed triumphantly, 'now we come to it! Dutch Royal family, are we?'

'Don't be so bloody stupid!' he growled.

'Who are you, then?'

'Well known,' he muttered.

'How well known?' Bryony persisted.

'Very well known!' he shouted.

'You said you weren't famous!' she accused.

'I'm not,' he denied impatiently, 'and you don't need to sound so damned suspicious! And——'

'If you aren't famous,' she continued obdurately, 'then——'

'Oh, for God's sake!' Dries exploded. 'The family's wealthy! We're all well known, all right? My father's a millionaire several times over. I'm wealthy, apart from inherited money from my grandparents, in my own field I'm something of an expert and can command a very high fee—but the point I was trying to make before you so rudely interrupted yet again is that Jan and Lilly, who are also disgustingly rich, and philanthropists to boot, also run a drug rehabilitation centre. He's currently in the States lecturing about addiction—and the whole pivot of his argument is that lack of parental control is often to blame!'

'Oh,' Bryony said lamely.

'Yes, oh! Look nice in print, that, wouldn't it? The experts' own daughter caught up in a drug scandal!'

'Which is why Clare said it,' she agreed. 'She thought it was the safest thing she could say because she assumed you'd do everything in your power to keep it quiet. That you'd whisk her back to school and make very sure that her parents didn't ever find out about it . . .'

'Yes,' he agreed tiredly.

'Only when you said you were going to report Daniel, she panicked . . .'

'Yes.'

'Poor Clare. Sad, isn't it? People who preach, put other people's houses in order, often forget about their own . . .'

'Yes,' Dries agreed flatly.

'Would you have reported it?' she asked, lifting troubled eyes to his.

'I don't know,' he sighed 'I wanted to kill Daniel. That's what frightens me. I might have . . .'

'Clare would have stopped it,' Bryony said quietly.

'I suppose so. I don't think I've ever felt so out of control. I think for a while I even wanted to kill you. When I came up to your room with Clare, you looked so——'

'Don't,' she said, turning away. 'I don't want to remember how awful I felt.'

'I said some terrible things to you,' Dries went on.

'Yes.'

'I didn't mean them.'

'You did at the time,' she pointed out.

'Only because . . . Oh, Bryony,' he sighed, 'why is it everything gets so complicated when you're around? Can't we start again?'

'No,' she murmured, shaking her head, determined

this time not to be stupid.

'Because you can't forgive me?'

'No.' She wished she'd said yes, only she found herself reluctant to lie. 'I understand why you said what you did, or at least I think I do. I'd probably have said the same—probably did,' she admitted honestly. 'But it has to finish here,' she said helplessly.

'Why?'

'Because it does!'

'Because you want a commitment?' Dries persevered.

'No, I don't want a commitment! I don't want anything—from anybody!'

'Not ever?' he asked in astonishment, 'You're intending to spend your whole life avoiding involvement? What happens when Daniel leaves home? As he will.'

'Nothing will happen!' she denied in exasperation, beginning to feel stupid and muddled. 'I'll go on as I am.'

'But why?' he asked, sounding so totally perplexed that Bryony panicked and said the first stupid thing that came into her head.

'Because I don't have time! I didn't ask you to pursue me—and I don't know why you are!'

'Yes, you do! I want you!'

'Well, you aren't going to have me!' she shouted childishly.

'Want to bet?'

'No, I don't want to bet! You're being ridiculous! All you feel is a mild attraction——'

'Oh, don't be so bloody stupid,' said Dries disgustedly. 'If it were only a mild attraction I wouldn't be making such a blasted fool of myself! Do you really think I enjoy behaving like a schoolboy? Do you? I don't know why I want you! But it fills my mind to the exclusion of all else! Oh, I sometimes think I want to rape you! Every damned movement you make arouses me, you know that, so at least have the decency to explain properly instead of pussyfooting all round the subject! And don't tell me you don't feel the same, because I know damned well you do!'

'I don't! I don't!' Bryony denied, her eyes wide and frightened as she stared at him, and all the old feelings of insecurity came tumbling back to swamp her. She didn't want to generate such violent feelings in anyone, didn't want to feel the way Dries was making her feel, didn't want it put into words, and she clapped her hands childishly over her ears as though it would make it all go away. She didn't want him to exude this raw power, this intensity, and yet against her will she felt her body change, became aware of the weight of her breasts, the drag in her abdomen. 'I don't,' she whispered.

'Don't you?' he asked relentlessly, his mouth pulled into a bitter line. 'Can you stand there and tell me honestly, hand on heart, that you feel nothing for me at all? That all you felt was passion brought on by a tropical moon? A flower-scented garden?'

'No, it wasn't like that, and I do like you——'

'Oh, thanks a lot! You're a damned little coward, Bryony, with a Peter Pan complex.'

'Maybe I am,' she admitted, too honest to deny the truth of his statement, 'but at least I don't try to browbeat someone into having an affair with me. And if I gave in? What then, Dries? You'd satisfy your lust and then wave goodbye. Well, I couldn't cope with that, I told you. I don't want to be hurt.'

'It doesn't have to end in hurting,' he denied, but he didn't sound very convinced, and she gave a sad smile. 'There's a very real possibility that it might end in laughter.'

'No, and you don't believe that any more than I do —and please don't tell me that you've remained friends with all your past mistresses,' she said tartly, 'because I don't want to know! Certainly I have no wish to join their ranks! Leave it be, Dries, please,' she pleaded wearily.

'And that's it?' he asked harshly. 'You can put your feelings into cold storage and they'll stay there?'

'Yes,' she agreed miserably, praying it might be true. 'I'm sorry.'

Dries stared at her, his expression grim, and the blue eyes that had so often softened in humour, in teasing laughter, looked like blue ice. The generous mouth was a tight line and she felt her eyes blur with tears for what might have been—if she hadn't been a coward. 'I'm sorry,' she said again.

With an abrupt movement, he turned and left, and she winced as she heard one of the milk bottles crash over. The roar of his car accelerating away sounded over-loud. Staring down at her hands that were still agitatedly twisting the end of her belt, Bryony felt her bottom lip quiver and clamped her teeth over it. She truly hadn't known that Dries's feelings were so intense. And he was wrong, she didn't feel the same—she didn't! She just had this awful empty ache inside, an overwhelming desire to cry. Dragging a deep breath into her lungs, she squeezed her eyes tightly shut, then snapped them open in shock as she heard his car return, the screech of brakes as he came to an abrupt halt which was swiftly followed by the slam of his car door. With a funny little sound of distress she stared frantically around her as though seeking an escape route. She didn't have to let him in, though, did she? And the front door was shut; she'd heard it slam. Her breath held, her hands clasped in front of her, Bryony jumped like a scalded cat when Dries thrust through the door from the garden. He was breathing heavily, his broad chest rising and falling in swift movements, and with one long stride he reached her side and dragged her into his arms, his mouth fastening cruelly on hers. For long seconds she was too shocked to move, and it was Dries himself who recovered first. Dragging his mouth from hers, he crushed her impossibly tight, her head trapped in the angle of his shoulder.

'I'm sorry,' he muttered into her hair. 'I've been behaving like an animal. I can't bear to be thwarted,' he added on a muffled grunt of laughter before moving her away so that he could look down into her face. His eyes still seemed over-bright, but at least there was rueful humour lurking in their depths, and she gave him a shaky smile. 'You were quite right, you didn't ask me to feel like this—and I can't work out why I do. I never behave like this. Never. But I'm not giving up,' he cautioned, 'I've just decided on a different approach.'

'Oh, Dries!' she exclaimed helplessly. 'I can't cope with this, I really can't. I feel like a wet dishrag!'

'Oh, is that what it is?' he teased huskily. 'I couldn't quite identify it.' With a determined air that made her feel even more helpless, he reached down and swept a pile of magazines off the chair beside him and, gingerly lowering himself into it, he pulled her to sit on his lap. 'Now, tell me. Tell me why a beautiful, sexy lady like yourself has turned into such a coward. I will accept, reluctantly, that you don't have the same feelings I have and that you won't have an affair with me, and, although I'm not actually altruistic enough to hope that you'll one day meet someone who'll marry you out of hand, I'd like to know why my little friend Bryony is behaving like a fool. So tell me,' he persuaded softly.

Her eyes filling with tears at his gentle tone, Bryony sniffed and looked down. She could feel the tension in him through the hard thighs beneath her own, the way he was trying to regulate his breathing, could feel her own tension that locked her muscles until they ached. Afraid to look at him, she fiddled absently with a button on her shirt while she thought what to say, then make a comical little face of astonishment when it came off in her hand. 'See? I can't even keep a button on my shirt—what chance do you think I'd have trying to hold a relationship together?'

'Stop procrastinating,' he ordered. 'Begin.'

'Begin,' she muttered. Where? How to make him understand? How could she tell him of her desperate need to be loved? Her fear of rejection? That everyone who she had thought should or might love her always ended up disliking her? Being irritated by her? 'My parents didn't like me—I told you that, didn't I?' and when he nodded, she continued, 'They said I was disruptive, difficult, impossible to live with, and so I was.'

'But you didn't live with them much, did you? I thought you said you were away at boarding school?'

'I was, but before that, when I was quite small. I always wanted to paint, you see, draw, play with Plasticine. That's all I wanted to do, and they got impatient, irritated by the mess I seemed constantly to want to live in. Mother thought the nuns would sort me out, and to a certain extent I suppose they did. Certainly they wouldn't let me do anything that wasn't strictly educational—the times I got punished for drawing over my exercise books I can't tell you! And I did try to reform,' she murmured, her eyes sad as she remembered those difficult days, 'but it was as though, the more they forbade me to behave sinfully, as they called it, the more of an obsession it became. They sent nasty sneaky reports home to the parents, and the whole relationship just went from bad to worse, and when you're little, it matters. So very much,' she added softly almost under her breath. 'Anyway, the upshot of it was that when I was eleven I was sent to the local grammar school. I think my father thought that , as the majority of the teachers were male, I might get more discipline. Unfortunately the reverse was true, they seemed more than happy to cherish my passion for art. That of course drove Father into a fury——'

'But why?' Dries asked in perplexity. 'I should have thought he would have been delighted that you had such a talent.'

'Delighted?' she scoffed. 'Don't be daft! He was horrified. Rather Victorian, was my father—a woman's place is in the home and all that. He thought I'd do better learning domestic science—and if he thought it, then believe me that was best! The whole thing became impossible,' she sighed. 'A veritable battleground. I told you about their arguments, didn't I?' and when Dries nodded, she resumed sadly, 'What I didn't tell you was that they were usually my fault. Their rows were all about me. I wouldn't see reason; he wouldn't see reason; Mother wept. By the time I went away to university, the rift had become too wide to bridge. I suppose, looking back, it was maybe a case of all of us being too stubborn to change or see the other's point of view. I stupidly thought that if I tried hard enough, long enough, they would come to love my drawing as much as I did.'

'But they didn't.'

'No, so I found digs in St Andrews that I could stay

in during the long holidays. I worked evenings in a pub, weekends on the check-out till of a supermarket. I managed, made some friends.'

'But you didn't go home,' said Dries.

'No. I pretended I was happy, fulfilled.' Giving a wry shrug that in no way banished the shadows from her eyes, Bryony continued, 'When they put the rent of my bedsit up, I went to share a house with some other girls—and I know I go off into daydreams, flit from one thing to another without seeming purpose, but I've found over the years that it's impossible to discipline myself, because the moment something else more interesting comes along I'm off. I know that, so it was inevitable, I suppose, that bit by bit I drove the girls I was sharing with insane. I'd get absorbed in what I was doing, drawing, a project, whatever, and forget it was my turn to do the cleaning or cooking. Their amused tolerance very rapidly turned to exasperation, then fury—quite rightly, of course—then I was asked to leave. So I found another bedsit—and I met and fell in love with Giles.'

With a small sad smile she continued reminiscently. 'At first it was wonderful, being in love and everything, having someone who seemed to understand me, and if I loved someone then I'd make an extra-special effort, wouldn't I?'

'I doubt it,' Dries muttered on a snort of laughter, 'but go on.'

'Well, I thought I would,' she qualified, because she had wanted so much to be loved, have someone of her own. 'I moved into his flat—and . . .'

'You told me you were an innocent,' Dries put in softly, and she gave him a wary glance.

'I know. That was because—well, I thought . . .'

'If I thought you totally innocent, I would behave?'

'Something like that,' she muttered, embarrassed. 'I didn't want you to think me a tease. I'm sorry, I'm not very experienced, there was only Giles that I—well, slept with.'

'All right, go on—and there's no need to look as though I'd caught you with your hand in the cookie jar. I forgive you. I might not like it,' Dries added with a rather odd smile, 'but I promise not to hold it against you.'

'Well, excuse me,' she said, turning to give him a haughty little glance that made him grin, 'after the things you accused me of, I should hope you wouldn't hold it against me!'

'All right, you can get off your high horse. I'll apologise most humbly later if that's what you want, only can we get on with the tale? If you keep distracting me I'll forget where we've got to—you moved into his flat . . .' he prompted.

'Yes. And I did try, Dries, I really did try!' Bryony explained earnestly as though he might not believe she tried at anything. 'In the beginning, I'd shop, get a meal ready for him, clean the flat, only—well, I had exams coming up, projects to prepare—and six weeks later he asked me to move out. He said it was like living with a blow-up doll. I looked human, but I obviously hadn't been programmed for communication or memory.'

Catching the amused twitch of his lips that Dries tried to conceal, she smiled sadly back. The memory still hurt, she found, the feelings of inadequacy and guilt. 'I anguished over it for ages. I really had thought I loved him.' Sighing, she said, 'I sound like a real moaning Minnie, don't I? I didn't mean to , I was just trying to explain how impossible I am to live with.

How afraid I am to try again——Oh, Dries, don't look at me like that!' she exclaimed worriedly as she noticed the way he was watching her.

'How am I looking?' he queried.

'You know! Sort of angry, and caring,' she mumbled awkwardly. 'And you mustn't.'

'No,' he agreed absently. 'Go on.'

Staring back down at her linked hands, Bryony took a shaky little breath. 'When Grandfather died, then the parents and Daniel came to live with me, that more or less put paid to any social life, and, although I know Daniel loves me, even he gets thoroughly irritated at times by my behaviour. When I finished at university, we moved down to London, rented another poky flat in Islington, and I worked hard trying to find markets for my work. That's how I met David,' she explained with a funny little grimace. Hadn't she told herself and told herself not to get involved with him? Hadn't she known how it would end? 'He owned a little art shop and agreed to take some of my models. He was nice,' she said lamely. 'He asked me out, and like a fool I agreed, but by about the fifth time I forgot to meet him, or was impossibly late for an appointment, he got pretty fed up about it, and then he too disappeared into the sunset. So I decided, no more serious relationships, no more hurt.'

'How long ago was that?' asked Dries.

'Two years.'

'I see.'

'Do you?' she asked quietly, turning once more to look at him. She hoped he did, hoped he saw how impossible it would be, hoped he would leave so that she could try and put him out of her mind, squash the silly little daydreams that caught her unawares at odd moments. Squash the feeling of warmth and desire he generated just by being there.

'I can see it would be a problem,' he agreed softly, 'but just because two men and an insensitive family didn't understand you, couldn't allow you to be yourself, it doesn't mean that no one else will. Oh, Bryony, stop looking so bewildered, it isn't your fault! It's theirs!'

'Of course it isn't,' she exclaimed weakly, 'it's mine! Haven't you understood one word of what I've said?' she demanded, shifting on his lap so that she could look fully into his face. 'I'm impossible to live with!'

'Rubbish,' he retorted. 'And will you please sit still?' he commanded with a tense smile.

'Sorry,' she muttered thickly, her cheeks flushed as she realised what he meant, 'and it isn't rubbish,' she denied quickly. Heaven knew, it had taken her long enough to come to terms with it, and to have him query it, and for her to even marginally entertain that query would only lay her open to more hurt, and she simply wasn't going to allow herself to do that.

Should she get up? she wondered. Move? It was becoming harder and harder to think straight, being so close to him. 'I know what I'm like,' she insisted, fighting to retain her composure, then stamped her foot when Dries snorted. Unable to bear the proximity any longer, she forced herself to stand upright and walk casually, or she hoped it looked casual, across to the bench, only to begin fiddling with a piece of hardened clay. Taking a deep shaky breath, she turned determinedly to face him.

'It doesn't mean I don't care for people. I do. But . . .'

'But it has to be on your terms.'

'Yes! I don't mean it to be that way, but that's how

it turns out. I know it's selfish, but I can't change—
I've tried.'

'Have they?' Dries asked softly.

'What?'

'Have they? These men who've professed to love
you, have they tried to understand? Change?'

'Why should they?' Bryony demanded in
astonishment.

'Why should *you*?'

Staring at him, her face a study in confusion, she
stuttered, 'Because it has to be a partnership, not
one-sided, because they would have to do all the giving.'

'Nonsense! There's such a word as compromise,
you know.'

'Of course there is! But I can't.That's what I've
been trying to tell you. I mean to, I start out with that
intention, but then I forget.'

'Then you'll just have to find someone more
tolerant,' said Dries.

'Oh, funny, who the hell is going to be that tolerant?
How would you like it if you never had any clean
shirts? If there were never any clean sheets because
I'd forgotten to do the washing?'

'The situation wouldn't arise,' he said blandly. 'I
always send my things to the laundry, Next?'

'What do you mean next?' she queried.

'Give me some more instances.'

Gazing at him in exasperation, she tried to organise
her arguments in her mind, and if he thought she
couldn't think of instances he was in for a shock. 'All
right, supposing you wanted——'

'We've got to the personal, have we?' he asked with
soft suggestion.

'What?'

'You said "you", meaning me, not a hypothetical person.'

'I didn't—wasn't—oh, stop it! I was only trying to illustrate what I meant. If "he",' she said defiantly,'wanted to have a dinner party and I'd agreed to cook for it . . .'

'I—"he",' he corrected humorously, 'wouldn't ask, he'd get caterers in. Don't forget you've presumably been living together for some months and he's beginning to know your little failings.'

'Well, just suppose he couldn't get any caterers, it was too short notice or something,' she said shortly, 'what then?'

'All right, his guests arrive, you're oblivious of the day, or even the time, you're happily playing with your bits of clay or wood or paints, so he takes them into the lounge——'

'Which I'd forgotten to clean,' Bryony put in triumphantly.

'That you'd forgotten to clean,' Dries put in amiably, 'he would explain with his usual charm that——'

'How do you know he's got charm?'

'Because he's a lot like me,' he explained, giving her a pitying glance that made her grind her teeth. 'He would explain that his lady was a gifted artist and they would have to excuse the mess—and if they were really friends, they would accept that and muck in. However, bearing in mind that by this time he knows you very well, he'd probably have engaged the services of a cleaner—and,' he continued, entering whole-heartedly into the spirit of the thing, 'working on the assumption that you had in a moment of exuberance offered to cook the meal, he would no doubt find you in the kitchen carving carrots instead of scraping them——'

'Right!'

'—but being a highly efficient and thoughtful person he would already have arranged for a catering firm to be on standby—just in case his lady became absorbed in carrot carving!' Lifting one eyebrow at her, his beautiful eyes full of laughter, Dries waited for her next comment.

'You're being ridiculous and you know it!' Bryony said crossly. 'To out-think my peculiarities would cost you—him—a fortune!'

'Then you'd have to find someone with a fortune—like me.' He added softly, 'What's money for if not for spending?'

'That's not the point,' she began feebly, before becoming thoroughly diverted by his mention of a fortune. 'Have you?' she asked lamely. 'Got a fortune, I mean?' He'd said he was wealthy, but a fortune?

'Mm. Apart from my own money, unlike your grandfather, mine actually quite liked me and settled vast sums on all three of us, Jan, Greta and myself. Father didn't mind at all. You'd like my father, he's a bit like you.'

'Nobody's a bit like me,' Bryony denied.

'Now that, my darling girl, sounds suspiciously like boasting,' he said on a laugh.

'It isn't boasting,' she mumbled, then, looking at him helplessly, exclaimed, 'It wouldn't work, Dries! Really it wouldn't. You'd move in here, I'd get to like you too much and then you'd move out, and I'd be left hurting.'

'How do you know?' he queried.

'I just do, believe me, and I won't let myself like you any more than I do now. I won't!'

'Which means that there's a very real possibility that you will,' Dries said arrogantly. 'Feelings don't go away just because you want them to. I know, I've tried. The very first moment I set eyes on you I knew you were going to be trouble. I tried very hard not to like you—only you're not an easy person to ignore.' Getting to his feet, he walked across to stand in front of her. 'And don't tell me that feelings aren't reciprocated just because I want them to be. I already know that too. However, I won't badger you any more now,' he said gently, 'but think about what I've said, hm? I have some work to catch up on, and on which I'll try very hard to concentrate, but in a few days, Miss Bryony Grant, I'll be back—and then, if you still feel the same, I'll leave you in peace.' Tilting her chin up with one finger, he looked down into her eyes, then, with a faint smile that held more than a hint of tension and a sort of sadness, he bent and dropped a swift kiss on her mouth. 'Be good!'

Be good? She rarely got the opportunity to be anything else, Bryony thought sadly, but she did think about Dries's words—of course she did. Hope seemed to be fighting a continual war with common sense. Why did she have to like him so much? It would be a hell of a lot easier if she didn't. Then she gave a hollow laugh. Of course it would, because then the problem would never have arisen. She also seemed to spend her whole time wandering round the house picking things up, then putting them down again, thinking about Dries. She missed him, missed his stupid sense of humour, his smile, his sexy voice. He was like an amiable tank,

she thought half crossly, trundling all over her, leaving
tyre marks. And yet once or twice he hadn't been
amiable, had he? And he'd frightened the life out of
her with that recent display of naked emotion—even
just the thought of it made her tremble, and ache. There
seemed to be an emptiness and yearning inside her that
no amount of resolution would dispel—and he didn't
phone. Five days passed, and no call. Had he thought
better of it? Realised that she'd been telling the truth?
That she was impossible to live with? But if he'd
thought that, he'd have come and told her, wouldn't
he? The sensible half of her told her to be glad, the
unsensible part sent her upstairs to shower and change
into clean jeans and T-shirt, grab her purse, and walk
along to the bus stop, because she needed to know.
Dries had put the hope in her heart and now it refused
to die.

As she walked along the lane towards the house
Bryony had a sense of *déjà vu*. The red car was parked
in exactly the same place, the weeds were as weedy,
the house as abandoned-looking as it had been then.
Was it really only two weeks ago? Walking up to the
front door, as she had then, she knocked hesitantly, and
it swung soundlessly open. Not normally given to
fears of the unknown, she nevertheless in this instance
felt a shiver go through her. It seemed too silent,
almost contrived. Telling herself not to be a fool, she
pushed the door wide and stepped inside—then gave
a long scream of fright as a cobweb-covered beam
dropped eerily down in front of her. Her heart beating
like a trip-hammer, her hand at her throat, she stared
at it in horror.
'What the hell is going on?' Dries thundered

furiously as he strode from the door at the end of the hall. He halted abruptly, his face wiped clean of expression, and then he looked—well, she didn't know how he looked, like a man who had just been given a very nasty shock. Had he been hoping she wouldn't come? she thought miserably. With what looked suspiciously like a shudder, he demanded, 'What are you doing here? Oh, hell, Bryony, this is not a good time.' Without waiting for her to answer he walked across to the wall the other side of the artistically draped cobweb and opened a panel. With the whisper of an electronic motor, the cobweb silently ascended.

'I don't like spiders,' she said defensively, wishing with all her heart that she hadn't come. Wasn't he even the least bit pleased to see her?

'There aren't any spiders,' he muttered disparagingly as he stared up at it, presumably to make sure she hadn't damaged it, she thought waspishly. 'It's an artificial web.'

'Well, artificial or not, it still nearly scared me half to death!' she retorted.

'Good. Pity we didn't think to record your scream, though . . .' Turning away from her, raking his untidy hair back with one very dirty hand, Dries called up the stairs, 'Harry? Did you hear that?'

'Yeah!' a voice floated back. 'Echoes beautifully.'

Giving a satisfied grunt, he turned back, then looked surprised to see Bryony still standing there. 'Oh, sorry,' he said offhandedly, 'you'd better come through—and for God's sake walk in the centre of the hall, or you'll set off everything else.'

Feeling hurt and unsure of herself, Bryony did as she was told. As Dries led the way through the door at the end of the hall, then threw himself into a battered chair behind an equally battered desk, she gave him a hesitant smile. 'I shouldn't have come, should I?'

'Well, I have to confess your timing could have been better—however, how are you?'

'I'm fine,' she said lamely. 'I——' then she broke off, startled, as the door burst open and a short thin man with sandy hair came thrusting in.

'Dries, where do you want this cable . . .? Oh, sorry,' he muttered with a lame smile, 'didn't know you had someone with you. Was it you who screamed?' he asked Bryony.

'Yes,' she admitted awkwardly. 'Sorry, did it . . .?' then for the second time she came to a lame halt as Dries leapt to his feet, exclaiming, 'George, where the hell did you get that cable?'

'It was up in the back bedroom,' George explained, looking totally confused.

'Oh, damn it! Who moved it? Harry, I'll bet it was Harry! I'll kill him!' Pushing past George, Dries strode from the room, yelling for the hapless Harry. Exchanging a bewildered glance with George, Bryony gave another lame smile.

'I seem to be somewhat in the way,' she apologised.

'Oh, I shouldn't worry about it,' he said kindly. 'Everyone's in the way this week. We can't get the lighting right. They want to start filming next week— some chance!' he exclaimed with a grin. 'Oh, well, back to the grindstone . . .' then he laughed when Dries's voice was heard yelling for him. 'Sorry, love, I have to go, nice to have met you.'

'And you,' she echoed. Staring round the empty little room, she debated whether to leave him a note, then, with an unhappy little shrug, decided better not.

It would probably turn out that she'd written on the lighting instructions or something. Neither did she fancy using the hall again, and, with a bewildered look around her, she went over to the window. Pushing up the sash, half terrified that some other prop would descend on to her luckless head, she scrambled out, then closed it behind her.

CHAPTER SEVEN

BRYONY stood in the lane staring blindly at nothing, feeling numb and very insecure. Dries had made it quite obvious that he no longer wanted her—although he had been busy, hadn't he? His mind had been elsewhere, but surely he could have at least pretended to be pleased to see her—— Then she broke off the thought midway. Why should he? She was doing to him what people usually did to her, wanting him to conform. To immediately drop what he was doing and give her his undivided attention; and, although it was galling to admit that he hadn't seemed exactly ecstatic at the sight of her, that didn't mean he was indifferent either, did it? If she went back home, she would be miserable—might as well be miserable here as there, mightn't she? Yes, she decided. Retracing her steps, she halted beside Dries's car. She'd wait here for a little while—and if he didn't come out? Refusing to admit to that possibility, Bryony gave the bonnet a little pat and leaned back against it and stared up at the sky. It wasn't so sunny today—was that an omen? How long should she wait? An hour? Less would seem not giving it a fair chance, and more would denote desperation—and she wasn't desperate, was she? Oh dear, she thought she was! Blanking out that thought, she stared resolutely at the waving grasses. Had she felt this intense over Giles and David? She didn't honestly think she had. Chewing worriedly on her lower lip, she came to the horrifying conclusion that she was behaving like a groupie; then giggled nervously at the terminology. A twenty-seven-year-old groupie?

'And what's amusing you, Miss Grant?' Dries asked softly from beside her, making her jump.

Turning her head, Bryony stared at him, totally unaware how lost and bewildered she looked. 'You shouldn't creep up on people like that,' she reproved faintly, then gave a reluctant smile at the ridiculous image he presented. His dark blond hair was sticking up in endearing spikes, there was a smudge of dirt across one cheekbone and he held a thick sandwich in one hand, a cup of something in the other—and she didn't want to take her eyes away from him, wanted to burrow against that solid chest, wanted to burst into tears.

Giving her a rather absent smile, he asked, 'Have you eaten?' and when she shook her head, he balanced his cup on the roof of his car and broke the enormous sandwich in half and handed her a piece. Taking it, knowing she'd never be able to force it past her dry throat, Bryony lifted the top section in a delaying tactic and looked dubiously at the contents.

'Is it ham?' she asked in a small voice, quite unable to identify the strange-looking piece of meat.

'Lord knows, it tastes all right. Gavin made it,' he added as though that would automatically clarify things.

'Oh well, if Gavin made it,' she murmured, having not the faintest idea who Gavin might be. Putting the top back on, she took a small experimental bite.

Settling himself beside her so that the car gave a protesting groan, Dries commented with apparent casualness, 'I thought you'd gone.'

'No. Well I did,' she explained honestly, 'but I came back.'

'So I see. And you didn't explain what was amusing you.'

'I was trying to decide if I was behaving like a groupie,' she said, with such seriousness that he gave a faint smile.

'And were you?' he asked gently.

'I don't know, I hadn't got that far, but I think I decided I was perhaps a bit too old to be one. How are you keeping?' she asked rather foolishly, because she could see how he was keeping: fine.

'Busy. I didn't phone you because—well, because telephone conversations are always so unsatisfactory,' said Dries, sounding so evasive that she looked miserably away. 'I've been rushing to finish here, but Murphy's Law's been operating to its most exasperating extent, and now they inform me that they want to start filming next week. Why did you come?' he asked bluntly.

'I don't know,' Bryony mumbled, then gave a funny little smile. 'I don't know how to behave any more, what to do—silly, isn't it? I even cleaned the house.'

'Did you?'

'Yes. I'd better get back, hadn't I? Let you get on.' When he didn't answer, she looked at him, only to find he was frowning down at the toe of his shoe, but not seeing it, she knew. Some problem was tugging at his mind and he was only giving her a fraction of his attention. Unable to resist the temptation, she laid her hand gently on his arm, then snatched it back as he glanced at her.

'Mm? Oh, sorry, Bryony,' he apologised with a

helpless shrug, 'but something that should work doesn't, and I can't for the life of me understand why. It's irritating me—it has to be a blue filter, I know that, so why won't it damned well work?' he muttered to himself, his gaze once more abstracted as he stared towards the house.

'I don't know. I don't know much about filters.' Letting her breath out on a little sigh, Bryony got to her feet. 'Goodbye, Dries,' she said softly, a little catch in her voice, but she doubted if he even heard her.

As she waited for the bus, she examined her feelings, really examined them, not pushed them away as she usually did, hoping they'd go away. 'A quite massive case of self-deception,' she told herself out loud. 'You've been in love with him for days. Yes. Possibly ever since the first time you met him. Yes. How could you be in love with someone you'd only known two weeks? She didn't know, she only knew that it was true. Seeing Dries again had proved that beyond a shadow of a doubt. She was shaking, inside and outside. She wanted him. Wanted to take what was offered and let tomorrow take care of itself. He'd once found her sexy and funny, hadn't he? Not that there'd been much humour in any situation lately, but could she make him feel like that again? Perhaps if she told him she was willing to have an affair? How awful to be so desperate, like one of those women she'd read about in the papers, chasing a man who didn't want her. Maybe if she smartened herself up a bit, took trouble with her hair . . . As the green bus ground to a halt beside her and the doors whispered open, she stared at the driver, who stared blandly back. 'What do you do,' she asked solemnly, 'if you've just discovered you're in love with someone?'

'Go and tell them?' he offered hopefully.

'Yes, but supposing he doesn't want that? Supposing he only wants . . .'

'Sex?' he asked

'Yes.'

'Well, what's wrong with that? Are you getting on or staying there?'

'Staying here,' she suddenly decided. He was right, what the hell was wrong with that? Giving the bus driver a wide, warm smile that made him catch his breath, she turned away to trudge back up the lane. But supposing Dries didn't want sex either?

He was still leaning against the bonnet of his car, the half-eaten sandwich still in his hand. Walking over, Bryony stood in front of him and waited to be noticed. She didn't have to wait very long. Turning his head, he stared at her, his blue eyes wary, and she frowned.

'Back again?' he asked with that same air of indifference.

'Yes,' she said firmly. 'I asked the bus driver's advice and he said what the hell was wrong with sex?'

'And what did you say?'

'That I didn't think there was anything wrong with it, and he said I should tell you.'

'Wise man,' he murmured. 'So tell me.'

'I want you,' she said in a little rush.

'Good. Is this a short-term project? Or a long-term project?' he added.

'I don't know,' she admitted faintly, thoroughly bewildered by his casual reception of her declaration. 'You don't mind?'

'No,' and for a moment his voice sounded rusty. Tossing the remains of his sandwich away, he drew her between his thighs with a fierce movement that startled her. 'I'm sick to death of cold showers,' he said savagely, 'I'm grubby and sweaty and I have forty million things to do—and none of them are more important than making love to you.' Pulling her yet closer, one large hand transferring to the nape of her neck, he took a deep breath, then fastened his mouth on hers in fierce hunger.

With a little sob of relief, Bryony wound her arms round his neck, held him tight and kissed him back with a passion that astonished her—and Dries, judging by the strangled moan he gave. Forcing her body as close to his as she could get, she pressed small urgent kisses on his mouth, his eyes, his cheeks, then back to his lips, and they exchanged a long, beautiful drugging kiss that melted her bones— then Bryony jerked upright as a long, piercing wolf-whistle shattered the stillness.

'Gavin,' Dries muttered thickly, and, as if to emphasise the fact that they weren't exactly in the best place for making love to each other, it began to rain, slow, heavy drops that soaked them in seconds. Taking her hand, he urged her round to the back of the house and in through the french doors, then pulled her back into his arms, his mouth finding hers with renewed urgency. Crushed to him, she wriggled closer, her arms tight round his neck, her toes barely reaching the floor. She felt hot, and fluid, her breathing laboured, and she wanted him so much she felt ill. How had she not known how much she wanted him? When he pulled her T-shirt from her jeans and slid his warm palms to her bare back, she shivered and pressed closer, sliding her fingers into his thick hair, then groaned deep in her throat as his thumbs found the sensitive spots in her spine.

'You aren't wearing a bra,' he croaked.

'No.'

'Oh, Bryony, I . . .' he muttered.

'Dries? We're going out for a pint! Be about an hour!' someone shouted. Gavin? George?

'Yo!' Dries called back, his voice distorted, then, taking a shuddering breath, he lifted Bryony into his arms, carried her to the couch and collapsed backwards on to it, Bryony still cradled to his chest. 'Your T-shirt's wet,' he grated. 'I think you should take it off,' and with a movement too swift to evade, even had she wanted to, which she didn't, he pulled it over her head, then shrugged out of his own shirt before rolling to cover her, sucking his breath in sharply as her naked breasts touched his broad chest. With a funny little growl, he forced his knee between her thighs, grasped her chin in strong fingers and turned her face up to his waiting mouth. It was a kiss that dragged deep at her soul, a kiss unlike any other he had given her, almost violent, yet not hurting her in the least, only demanding an equally violent response. Her fingers digging into his back, she arched beneath him, forcing his thigh deeper into her groin as she sought to find fulfilment in his desperate kisses. From her jaw, his hand slid swiftly past her shoulder to cradle the side of her breast, his thumb reaching, finding the hard peak, and her breath jerked in her lungs, her teeth involuntary sinking into his lower lip.

'You took your time, didn't you, wretched girl? I've been going spare,' gasped Dries, his voice husky and unnatural, his glance almost feverish.

'I thought you didn't want me.'

'Oh, I wanted you, I always have, but I was trying to persuade myself that I wasn't that desperate.'

'You looked horrified when I came.'

'Because I'd just realised something I should have known days ago—weeks ago.'

Not understanding any of it, wanting only to be kissed, made love to, Bryony pulled his head back down to hers. She wanted him, very, very badly, and her fingers dug into his back in a small involuntary spasm that transmitted her frustration to him.

'Oh, God, Bryony, I want you!' he gasped.

'Yes!'

Staring at each other, they both reached down at the same moment and there was an urgent, undignified scramble to get rid of their clothing. Heated flesh met heated flesh, making them both gasp, and then it was too late for thoughts, only feelings that threatened to riot out of control. Bryony could hear her own soft gasps and moans as Dries touched her, his movements feverish, his kisses desperate, short, hard kisses that punctuated his ragged breathing. His skin felt hot, damp, and it was taking too long—and the sofa was too narrow, and he was too heavy and too tall—or she was too short. Frustration at being unable to hold him properly made her curse softly under her breath as she touched him, held him, sank her teeth into his shoulder in agitated little gestures. 'Oh, please!' she moaned helplessly.

'I'm trying, dammit! Oh, God, this is ridiculous, it's like a wrestling match!' Rolling away from her, Dries grabbed his clothes. 'Get dressed!' he ordered savagely.

'But can't we on the floor . . .' she began, frustration and need making her voice shake, then she realised that a mouse would have had trouble doing anything on the floor; it was covered in debris—things spilling from boxes, arc lamps, coils of wire. Biting her lip, she scrambled into her clothes, then stood facing him, her breathing still agitated, her limbs trembling. There was a dry, hot feeling behind her eyes. 'I——' she began.

'Don't say anything!' he pleaded. 'Not one word!' Avoiding her eyes, he grabbed her hand and dragged her out to his car. Slamming the door on her, he got behind the wheel and drove far too fast back to her house. 'Inside!' he ordered.

'Fumbling her key out of her purse, Bryony tried to fit it in the door with a hand that shook violently, only to have it snatched impatiently out of her hand.

'Where?' Dries demanded, sounding brutal and impatient.

'Where what?' she asked helplessly.

'The bedroom, dammit!'

'Oh.' Leading the way upstairs, her jerky breathing now due to nerves, she silently pointed out her room. Shoving open the door, he swept her inside, then glanced in disgust at the single bed.

'Get undressed,' he said shortly.

'Dries, I——'

'Undressed!' he roared as he shrugged off his own clothes, and she gave a nervous giggle. 'And if you dare laugh . . .'

'No,' she gasped. 'No,' then she had to turn away as she felt a traitorous little bubble of laughter rise in her throat.

'God, I've never felt so embarrassed in my entire life!' he muttered.

'Oh, Dries, don't! It doesn't matter.'

'Yes, it does! And I told you to get undressed.'

'Yes, Dries,' she said meekly.'

Tugging her T-shirt over her head as he removed the rest of his clothing, she gasped as she saw the strength of his arousal, and warmth flooded into her stomach, her nipples hardening in anticipation.

It wasn't a gentle union, but then she hadn't expected it would be after the way Dries had behaved. He took her without any preliminaries, his breathing harsh, his body hard as it thrust into hers—yet she was more than ready to receive him, and there was an urgent, overwhelming need to prove that her feelings were every bit as desperate as his own. Holding him tight, barely able to breathe for his weight crushing her, she fought to anticipate his needs, and an involuntary cry escaped her as she climaxed, too soon, too soon, she thought frantically, then groaned in relief as he shuddered, finding his own release. As he slumped weakly she trailed soothing, feverish kisses across his damp chest, murmured words that had no meaning. Every part of her ached, inside and out; she felt light-headed, reckless, and gloriously satiated as she lay quiet, savouring for the moment his weight, his warmth. When he stirred and rolled away from her she stared up at the ceiling, and as her mind began to function again she began to wonder what happened next. Moving only her eyes, she peeped towards him. He too was staring upwards, his face expressionless.

'Dries?' she whispered.

'Don't,' he groaned. 'God, what a fiasco!'

'The last part wasn't,' she denied softly, 'or not for me.'

'Wasn't it?' and he sounded so miserable, so

hesitant that she jack-knifed into a sitting position and stared down at him in astonishment.

'You need reassurance?' she asked incredulously.

Moving his eyes to hers, Dries gave a reluctant, muffled laugh, and she slapped him.

'What on earth made you get a stupid miniature bed?' he asked in disgust, thumping the mattress so hard that the springs twanged in protest.

'Because I'm little and I didn't know I was going to make love to a Dutch giant!' she protested, collapsing back on to the pillow, embarrassed now at her nakedness, at the abandon she'd shown.

'No,' he murmured, moving to lean up on one elbow, 'and I'm only half Dutch.' Capturing a strand of her hair, he twisted it round and round his finger. He looked wary, Bryony saw, and she frowned. Why was he wary? Because he was trying to think of a way to leave without upsetting her? 'Remind me never, ever, to attempt seduction on a sofa again. I've never felt so humiliated in my entire life!' he said flatly.

'Well, it wasn't exactly comforting for me either,' she pointed out, turning her head to give him a hesitant smile.

'No. I'm sorry.'

'Oh, don't apologise,' she gabbled. 'I wouldn't have missed it for the world. How are the mighty fallen!'

'Yeah,' he agreed with a rueful smile. 'Is that what you wanted, Bryony? To see me humbled?'

'No,' she denied. What she wanted was to know what happened now. Did he just get up and go? Did she? Offer to make a cup of coffee? Tea?

With an odd smile that she couldn't even begin to interpret, Dries suddenly stiffened, his eyes going wide with shock as he grabbed his watch from the bedside table. 'Oh, my God, it's five o'clock!' he exclaimed.

'Is it?' she asked, bewildered. 'Good heavens!'

With a little grunt of laughter that sounded quite false, he kissed her nose. 'The filter, wretched girl! I have to finish the filter.'

'Oh,' she said lamely. 'I'd forgotten the filter.'

'Yes, so had I. Bryony, I'm sorry, but I have to go.'

'Yes, of course you do,' she encouraged, trying to sound more positive than she felt. 'I'll see you later, I expect, shall I?'

'Yes, of course,' he murmured, but he had gone away from her, she knew; his voice was absent, his expression distracted as his mind moved on to obviously more important things.

Trying desperately not to let the hurt show, Bryony smiled widely, 'Go on, off you go,' she told him, 'the men will wonder where you've got to.'

'That's not all they'll wonder,' he said with a wry grimace as he scrambled from the bed and began dragging on his clothes with what she privately thought was indecent haste.

'No, but I expect you'll cope.'

'Yes. You're all right?' he asked, turning to face her.

'Yes, of course—I'm fine. Go on, go and finish playing with your filters.'

'OK. Thanks Bryony.' Grabbing his car keys from the dresser, Dries made for the door, then turned back unexpectedly. Striding to the bed, he bent and kissed her hard. 'I'm sorry,' he apologised again, and then he was gone.

Sitting up and stuffing the pillow behind her, Bryony hugged her knees. He hadn't even said if he'd enjoyed it, she thought miserably. Hadn't said when he would be back. Had it not meant anything to him? Just a release from frustration? Laying her head on her updrawn knees, she allowed tears of self-pity to fall. She'd wanted to hold him, snuggle up against his warm body, talk, make plans . . . With a surge of impotent misery, she dragged the pillow out from behind her and hurled it at the wall. Giles had said she was odd at times, behaved erratically, but even he had never rushed off with quite such alacrity after making love the way Dries had done. Had he been so very disappointed?

Oh, Bryony, stop it! she scolded herself. You knew it was a snatched moment, knew it was only want for him, a release from frustration. When did he ever promise anything more? With a long sigh, she scrubbed her tears away with her fists, then went into the bathroom to have a shower. It didn't seem worth getting dressed, she'd probably have an early night, so she slipped into a cotton nightdress with a Save the Whale slogan across the front; she might as well save somebody, she thought despondently—she sure as hell didn't seem to be having much success saving herself. So sure, weren't you? she mocked herself. That you only had to be firm, only had to say no. With a rather forlorn smile, she wandered downstairs. She supposed she ought to eat something—not that she felt hungry, but wasting away wouldn't solve anything. Staring blindly at the toaster, she suddenly screwed her eyes tight shut and locked her breath hard in her lungs to stop her tears. 'Oh, Dries,' she whispered brokenly, 'what have you done to me? What in God's name have you done?' She didn't think he'd come back.

Deciding that after all she couldn't face food, she

went into her workshop. Perhaps if she involved herself in something it would take her mind off Dries, take away the awful ache inside her.

Picking up her sketchpad, she idly leafed through it until she came to the one she had done of the Malay gardener, and, fiercely blocking out the memories of the evening she had drawn it, she stared at it critically. It actually seemed as good as she remembered, which wasn't always the case, and without really thinking about it she went to the cupboard and collected the tangle of wire she used to make a framework. Snipping off a length, she sat at the bench and began to bend it into shape, then, sticking the ends into a wooden base, she reached over to drag the bin of clay towards her. It didn't take long to cover the wire frame and outline the general shape, and, settling herself more comfortably into her chair, she forced herself to concentrate—and gradually, bit by bit, the image of Dries faded as she became engrossed in transforming her original drawing into the actual figure.

As always when she was absorbed, she didn't notice the passing of time, didn't notice anything outside the immediate circle of her concentration, not the rain hurling itself at the window, nor the opening of the back door and the entry of the wet and dishevelled figure of Dries. Didn't see the warm, loving smile he gave her clay-daubed figure nor hear him softly close the door and lean tiredly back against it. Her lower lip caught between her teeth, her eyes distant, Bryony used all her senses to transmit the image in her mind on to the figure taking shape before her. When she was sure she had the drape of his garments as she wanted, she moved her hands away and leaned back. Staring critically at what she had done, she gave a little nod of satisfaction. It would do. She'd start on the features tomorrow. Her concentration broken, she became aware of how stiff her shoulders were, and with a wide yawn stretched her arms above her head —then froze, her arms still uplifted as she finally registered Dries's presence. He looked tired to death, and expressionless. Lowering her arms, she asked dazedly, 'How long have you been there?'

'Hours,' he lied softly.

'What time is it?'

'Two in the morning.'

Giving him a distracted smile, her mind unable to comprehend the fact that he was there, that he had come back, Bryony found she didn't know what to say, could only stare at him, and such an overwhelming feeling of love spread through her that she felt faint. Getting to her feet, she caught sight of her dirty hands and held them out to show him in an endearingly childlike gesture. 'I'd better wash them,' she said.

'Yes. And your face, you have a streak of clay across one cheek.'

With a jerky little nod, she walked across to the sink on legs that felt decidedly unsteady. She felt nervous and didn't know why, her heart too was beating unevenly as she washed her face and hands, then made a great production out of drying them, keeping her attention firmly on her task. Dries's coming back meant he must care too, mustn't it?

'What's wrong?' he asked quietly. 'Changed your mind? Decided you want to opt out?'

'No,' she said, too quickly, then bit her lip and shook her head vigorously, 'No.' Taking a deep breath, she

hung up the towel and looked at him, her eyes clear
and honest. 'I haven't changed my mind, I just didn't
know what to say, what you expected, and seeing you
standing there I was suddenly afraid.'

'Why?' he asked.

'Because— well, because,' she mumbled lamely.
She couldn't tell him she loved him so much it was
killing her, could she? He didn't want her to love him;
he'd said so, in Singapore.

'You didn't think I'd come back, did you?' he said.

'No.'

'Come here,' he ordered softly.

Swallowing drily, Bryony walked towards him, and
gave a soft little sigh as he drew her against him and
held her close. 'I'd wanted you for such a long time,
Bryony. It might have only been time measured in
weeks, but it felt like the whole of my life. I'd been
holding myself in check to the very limit of my
endurance, and when you came to the house my
feelings just spiralled out of control and I behaved like
a crass schoolboy. First the fiasco of the settee, then
not being able to wait on that silly narrow bed—I felt
embarrassed and stupid. The one time when it was so
very important, I failed.'

'No, you didn't'

'Be quiet, let me finish. You were trying so hard to
make everything seem special, good, and I could see
by your face that you just felt bewildered, and I kept
thinking, oh, my God, she doesn't know how to tell
me to take a hike, so I——'

'No!' she protested, trying to wriggle free so that
she could see his face, only to have his arms tighten
and hold her still.

'So I grabbed my watch,' Dries continued strongly,

'said the first stupid thing that came into my head, and made a run for it.'

'But you had to get back to sort out the filter——'

'Don't be stupid, Bryony—filters were the last damned thing on my mind. Neither were they very much on my mind when I got back to work. If George and Harry hadn't been used to the way I work, hadn't been able to interpret my drawings, we'd never have got the job finished. As it was, it took twice as long as it should have done.' Letting his breath out on a sigh, he rubbed one hand absently up and down her back. 'On the drive over here I kept telling myself, she'll be in bed, fast asleep, and won't be in the least bit pleased at being woken up. Or she'll laugh in your face, or——'

'Shut up, Dries!' Oddly, now that he seemed unsure, Bryony could be strong. Forcing herself away from him, she stared into his tired face. 'I didn't think any of those things,' she denied gently, then with a teasing little smile, she admitted, 'I kept wondering what I was supposed to say, if I should offer you a cup of tea . . .' She giggled enchantingly. 'I thought you were eager to get away because you were disappointed.'

'No. Oh, no!'

'Then stop talking and take me to bed, please. I'm very, very tired.'

Giving a little nod, humour once more lurking in his beautiful eyes, Dries swung her up into his strong arms. 'But first thing tomorrow, we're going to buy a great big bed,' he told her.

'OK,' she smiled.

Carrying her upstairs to her room, he laid her on the quilt and stared down at her for a moment. 'Want to sleep?' he asked.

'No. Do you?'

'No.'

Feeling a funny little shiver go through her, Bryony dragged off her nightdress, then leaned across to the lamp and switched it on. 'I want to see you,' she said huskily.

'Oh, hell!' With a crooked smile, Dries undressed, then gave a self-mocking laugh. 'I don't think I've ever met anyone who ties me up in knots like you do, Bryony Grant! Shove over.'

Wriggling to the side of the narrow bed, she kept her eyes fixed on him as he gingerly balanced himself beside her.

'I'm almost afraid to touch you,' he murmured, running one large palm from her knee to her breast, and her nipples hardened in anticipation. 'You're such an exquisite little thing—fragile.'

'I'm not in the least fragile,' she denied, rolling to meet him, then groaned as her body touched his. Closing her eyes, she stretched against him, her hands fluttering like small birds over his chest, sighed as warm palms traced her shape, burrowed close to his hard body, found his mouth with hers. As he rolled to cover her, his forearms supporting his weight, she gave a muffled giggle, and he straightened his arms and stared down at her.

'I'm being squashed!' she protested with an infectious laugh, her beautiful eyes full of mirth, 'I only weigh seven and a half stone and you must be at least twice that, and right at this moment,' she added, her eyes growing darker, her voice softer, 'I surely don't want to be squashed.'

'Only to taste a bit of heaven?' he asked unevenly.

When she nodded, he knelt and sat back, her legs trapped between his, and she drew in her breath sharply at the magnificence of him.

'Oh, Dries,' she whispered, 'you're so beautiful,' and, without thinking what she was doing, she slid her hands up his hard-packed thighs towards his groin until a low groan escaped him.

'Oh, hell, Bryony, don't do that!'

'Why?' she pleaded, her voice sounding strangled. 'I want so much to touch you, and you're too far away.' Dragging a deep, steadying breath into her lungs, she tugged him to lie beside her, then scrambled to sit across him 'This is the way little people make love to giants,' she whispered throatily, her eyes fixed on his. With a shuddering sigh, she moved her aching body to cover him. Her eyes closed, her neck stretched, she blindly put out her hands to touch his chest, then felt her breath lock in her throat as his warm palms moved to cover her breasts.

'How do you know?' he groaned. 'Had lots of practice?'

'No, I just made it up——Oh, God, don't talk.'

'No.' Sliding his hands to her shoulders, he pulled her slowly towards him and held her cradled to his chest, his palms smoothing down over her waist to her buttocks, his breathing laboured—and they both found it worked very well. More than well, it was beautiful, slow, exciting, and Bryony's heart swelled with love for this big man that she had fought for so long to keep at a distance. He tasted of sun, she thought hazily, of warmth and safety, and as the rhythm changed, accelerated, thoughts were suspended and she clasped him tight, held him, cried his name, every part of her reaching out for that final ecstasy.

His breathing still heavy and slow, his movements

lethargic, Dries eased her gently along his magnificent body, then turned her to lie beside him, his arms holding her close. 'Open your eyes,' he instructed huskily.

'Why?' she whispered.

'Because I want to see how you feel.'

'You know how I feel,' she sighed, lifting lids that felt too heavy. 'I feel lazy and languorous and aching. Oh, Dries, that was so beautiful!'

'Yes, it was,' he agreed.

Staring bemusedly up into his face, Bryony slowly examined the flush that lay along his cheekbones, searched eyes that seemed a brighter blue, then asked quietly, 'How do you feel?'

'Like a man wanting desperately to surrender his freedom,' he confessed seriously.

'What?' she asked in disbelief.

'You heard. The minute I walked into the hall of the house and found you staring at me through a cobweb I knew—and I was suddenly terrified that you'd come to tell me to get lost. That was also why I behaved like a moron later, sitting against my car, a last-ditch attempt at self-preservation. I still didn't know why you'd come, didn't know what to say, so I sat like a fool with an unwanted sandwich in my hand and pretended a distraction I was very far from feeling.'

'Oh, Dries!' she whispered.

'Besides,' he continued, his voice ragged with emotion, 'if I don't grab you, Gavin promised to move in for the kill—he said you were the sexiest little thing he'd ever seen, and so you are. I want you, Bryony—I want you for keeps—I want to marry you. I don't want anyone else to ever touch you, feel what I feel. Oh, darling, don't cry! Is it so very terrible for me to be in love with you?'

Shaking her head, unable for the moment to speak through the lump in her throat, Bryony put her hand out blindly to touch him. 'No—oh, Dries . . .' and, burrowing against his strong chest, she mumbled shakily, 'I didn't know, I thought . . .'

'You won't marry me, is that it?'

'No!' she exclaimed, jerking away from him and staring at him in horror. 'No! Yes, I mean yes! Yes, I will marry you, please . . .Oh, Dries, I've been in love with you for ages—why else do you think I came to the house?'

'You said——' he began.

'I know what I damned well said!' she shouted, her exquisite face reflecting her joy and relief, 'but you said——' then she subsided with a muffled grunt as he put a hand over her mouth. He looked like a man gone into severe shock.

'You're in love with me?' he asked hesitantly, and she nodded frantically. 'You'll marry me?' and she nodded again, her eyes laughing at him over the barrier of his hand.

Grasping his wrist, she moved his hand away, then flung her arms round his neck. 'I love you, you great ox! Now you say it.'

'I love you——Oh, Bryony, I've been behaving like such a fool, haven't I?' With a soft, rueful smile, Dries traced a finger down her nose and across her lips. 'I'd never been in love before, you see, didn't think the state existed. It makes a hell of a difference, doesn't it? Because the outcome matters so much.' With a little laugh, he confessed, 'I owe my sister an apology—I seem to remember telling her to pull herself together when she was behaving like an idiot over some man.

Wait until it happens to you, she said. Not me, said I. Oh boy, her behaviour was sanity itself compared to mine! She'll laugh like a drain when I tell her.'

'Will you tell her?' she asked, intrigued.

'Of course. Think I'm ashamed of my feelings? Or of you?'

Shaking her head, Bryony smiled when he planted a kiss on her forehead. 'It won't be a very conventional partnership, will it?' she asked doubtfully, not sure she could fully believe him, afraid now that happiness seemed within reach that it would all go wrong.

'It certainly hasn't so far,' he said with a wide boyish grin, 'and having your beloved get a fit of the giggles when you're trying to make love to her seems only to confirm it.'

'I'm sorry,' she said penitently.

'Don't be. It adds a whole new dimension to making love.' His gaze growing sombre, he asked, 'Is that how it was with . . .?'

'No,' she whispered, tightening her hold fractionally. 'In fact, thinking back, they were both rather serious people. I don't think I ever felt happiness bubble up inside me whenever I was with them like I do with you. And anyway, it was only Giles. David didn't last long enough for us to become intimate. Oh, Dries, it will work, won't it?' she asked anxiously. 'I couldn't bear it if it all went wrong!'

'It won't, we won't let it.' Gently smoothing her hair back off her face, Dries smiled down at her. 'I love you. Whenever I just think of you I start to grin,' and, as if to confirm his words, his eyes creased with humour.

'I love you too, so very much.' Sliding one palm up his nape into his hair, her trembling fingers lingering in the thick strands, Bryony murmured softly, 'Did you know that your accent gets more pronounced when you're aroused?'

'Does it? Like it?'

'Mm, love it.'

'Better make sure I'm often aroused, then, hadn't you?' As they smiled at each other, Dries suddenly exclaimed, 'My God, they must have been insane to let you go!'

'Who?' she asked, bewildered.

'Giles, was it? And the art-shop person.'

'No,' she laughed, 'I expect they were very relieved.'

'Don't still see them, do you?' he asked rather too casually.

'No. Would it bother you if I did?'

'Yes,' he said simply. 'I'd like to pretend they never existed,' then he gave her an odd smile when she looked distressed, 'Sorry, not fair, was it?'

'No,' she said quietly.

'OK, subject closed.' With a change of mood he gave her a lazy grin and, burrowing into the pillow, commanded sleepily, 'You can tickle my back if you like.'

With a little snort of laughter Bryony flung one arm over his back and began describing small circles, her touch light.

'Mm, bliss—no, don't stop,' he protested when her movements stilled.

With a fond smile, she began smoothing her hand up and down his back, and within a few minutes he was asleep. Dragging the cover off the floor, she covered them and snuggled against his warm body, but it was a long time before she fell asleep. She wanted to savour the moments she found, relive them, and she touched his sleeping face almost reverently, still afraid to believe.

The early morning sun woke her and she lay for a while enjoying the warmth of Dries beside her, the heavy weight of his arm across her waist. Careful not to wake him, she reached down for the sketchpad and pencil that were on the floor, and, easing herself up until her back was against the headboard, she began to draw him. Pushing the covers down with her toes until she had uncovered him to the backs of his knees, she sketched in the outline.

'It's cold,' he mumbled.

'Nonsense, don't be a baby.' Looking down at him, at the one blue eye that was visible, the stubbled chin, she grinned. 'Boy, do you look rough!'

'You don't,' he murmured huskily. 'You look wholly delightful,' then smiled when she blushed. Reaching out an arm, he tilted the pad so that he could see what she was doing. 'That's rude!' he exclaimed, turning on his side so that he could see it properly.

'It is not! It's art.'

'No, it isn't, it's me naked! I hope you aren't intending for anyone else to see that.'

Spluttering with laughter, Bryony took the pad away and dropped it on the floor. 'No, it's for private consumption, as is this,' she growled, sliding down the bed to touch her body against him, then she drew her breath in sharply as she felt his body react to her nearness. 'You're——'

'Yes,' he agreed drily, 'you have that effect on me.' Pressing his nose to hers, he slipped his arms round her. 'Good morning. Can I expect to be woken like this every morning?'

'No. Some mornings I shall expect you to be the waker. Is it real?' she asked softly.

'Yes,' he confirmed, reaching out a hand to tangle his fingers in her hair, 'and as soon as we're up, which of course could take anything up to a week, maybe longer, we'll get dressed and go and see about making arrangements for the wedding, then we'll fly across to Belgium to see my parents——'

'I thought they lived in Holland?' she queried.

'No, Bruges. My father's family have lived there for generations.'

'Will they like me?' asked Bryony.

'Adore you,' he said with a small intimate smile. 'They're not all like Clare, you know.' Then, frowning slightly, he asked, 'Did I apologise for Clare?'

'Yes,' she confirmed softly, 'I expect she'll grow out of it. Seventeen is a very awkward age.'

'Mm,' he agreed, a doubtful smile in his beautiful eyes. 'Anyway, to continue: when my family have praised my cleverness in finding you, we'll decide where we're going to live—and make sure there's a very large bed there.'

'You have to travel a lot, don't you?' Bryony asked.

'Yes. Will that be a problem for you?' he asked with an endearing touch of hesitancy.

'No. I can work anywhere—and if you think, my lad, that I'll let you out of my sight, you're very, very mistaken!'

'And if you honestly thought I'd let you out of mine, then you're a fool,' Planting a warm, delightful kiss on her mouth, Dries added, 'If I make sure you always have a workshop and materials, it will be all right won't it?'

'Yes.'

'What else?'

'Daniel?' she asked hesitantly. 'He will be able to live with us, won't he? When he's home from university?'

'Oh, lord! Yes, I suppose so. I dare say we can come to some sort of arrangement—like his wearing a gag . . . Only joking,' he promised, grinning at her. 'It's more likely to be a case of will he live with me after the way I treated him. Anything else?'

'No,' she denied quietly.

'Then why are you looking so sombre?'

With a funny little sigh she traced a hesitant finger across his mouth. 'Fear, I suppose,' she mumbled, her eyes on her moving finger.'Doubts.'

'Because we haven't known each other very long?'

'No, it isn't that,' she denied slowly, her brow furrowed. 'I feel as though I've always known you. Funny, that, isn't it? From the first time I met you, I felt safe, happy. No, I'm just afraid you'll get fed up with me.' Lifting her lashes, she asked worriedly, her words a little rush of sound, 'Dries? I can be myself, can't I?'

'Aren't you always yourself?' he asked gently as he pushed the tumbled hair off her forehead.

'Yes, but sometimes when the demons come there's this great empty place inside me and I don't know who I am or what I am. It frightens me—and sometimes I just need to be held, not for anyone to say anything, just to be held. And if I exasperate you, you won't shout at me, will you?'

'Oh, darling, I promise not to shout at you,' he soothed, a little flicker of humour in his eyes.

'And I won't have to pretend, will I?' she went on.

'No.'

'But I had to tell you, didn't I? It wouldn't be fair to let you think I'm always happy and smiling, because it isn't true.' Scrambling to her knees, Bryony stared down at him, her beautiful face earnest. 'I'm not very brave sometimes, and when the demons come I do silly things, say silly things. . .'

'Now I'm beginning to think I don't know you at all,' said Dries with a loving smile. 'Intriguing. Tell me about the demons.'

'I don't know who they are or where they come from,' she sighed, 'they just come. Not often, I wouldn't want you to think that, but sometimes I feel so lonely, so sad.'

'Doesn't everyone feel like that sometimes?' he asked softly, pulling her back down to lie beside him. 'Shadows that creep up without warning?'

'It won't matter?'

'No, darling, it won't matter, but any relationship is a gamble. I can't make promises, I can only tell you how I feel now, how I think I'll always feel. You delight me, enchant me, make me laugh, make me feel protective. I have a great big ache inside for you. I want to love you and look after you, chase away your demons. I feel complete, fulfilled.'

'Yes,' she whispered, turning to smile at him. 'That's how I feel too. I don't want you to go away. I want to look up and find you there, to be able to touch you. . .' Staring into the strong face, she felt a lovely warmth fill her. 'You're so beautiful,' she whispered.

'And a genius,' Dries added with a teasing smile. 'You forgot to say genius.'

'Are you a genius?'

'Oh, yes. I found you, didn't I?'

'No. I found you.'

'Ah, but you were going to discard me. If it hadn't been for my persistence . . .'

'All right, I'll concede the point—but only if you make love to me,' Bryony added softly.

'Now?' Dries asked throatily, moving his lower body closer.

'Yes.'

'No problem. Geniuses are ready and able at all times.'

'Are they?' she smiled.

'Oh, yes!'

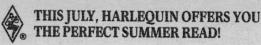

**THIS JULY, HARLEQUIN OFFERS YOU
THE PERFECT SUMMER READ!**

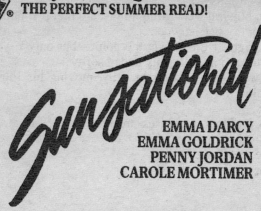

Sunsational

**EMMA DARCY
EMMA GOLDRICK
PENNY JORDAN
CAROLE MORTIMER**

From top authors of Harlequin Presents comes
HARLEQUIN SUNSATIONAL, a four-stories-in-one
book with 768 pages of romantic reading.

Written by such prolific Harlequin authors as Emma Darcy,
Emma Goldrick, Penny Jordan and Carole Mortimer,
HARLEQUIN SUNSATIONAL is the perfect summer
companion to take along to the beach, cottage, on your
dream destination or just for reading at home in the warm
sunshine!

Don't miss this unique reading opportunity.

Available wherever Harlequin books are sold.

SUN

Coming soon
to an easy chair near you.

FIRST CLASS is Harlequin's armchair travel plan for the incurably romantic. You'll visit a different dreamy destination every month from January through December without ever packing a bag. No jet lag, no expensive air fares and *no* lost luggage. Just First Class Harlequin Romance reading, featuring exotic settings from Tasmania to Thailand, from Egypt to Australia, and more.

FIRST CLASS romantic excursions guaranteed! Start your world tour in January. Look for the special **FIRST CLASS** destination on selected Harlequin Romance titles—there's a new one every month.

NEXT DESTINATION:
FLORENCE, ITALY

 Harlequin Books

JTR7

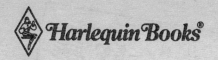

GREAT NEWS...

HARLEQUIN UNVEILS NEW SHIPPING PLANS

For the convenience of customers, Harlequin has announced that Harlequin romances will now be available in stores at these convenient times each month*:

Harlequin Presents, American Romance, Historical, Intrigue:

> May titles: April 10
> June titles: May 8
> July titles: June 5
> August titles: July 10

Harlequin Romance, Superromance, Temptation, Regency Romance:

> May titles: April 24
> June titles: May 22
> July titles: June 19
> August titles: July 24

We hope this new schedule is convenient for you.

With only two trips each month to your local bookseller, you'll never miss any of your favorite authors!

*Please note: There may be slight variations in on-sale dates in your area due to differences in shipping and handling.

HDATES-R

Back by Popular Demand

Janet Dailey
Americana

A romantic tour of America through fifty favorite Harlequin Presents® novels, each set in a different state researched by Janet and her husband, Bill. A journey of a lifetime in one cherished collection.

In June, don't miss the sultry states featured in:

Title # 9 - FLORIDA
        Southern Nights
    #10 - GEORGIA
        Night of the Cotillion

Available wherever Harlequin books are sold.